PEACEFUL SOCIETY
BOOK 1

PRIVILEGE

MEGAN WOBUS

In memory of Brigitte
aviator, activist, artist, mother
and writer

THE PEACEFUL SOCIETY TRILOGY

MEGAN WOBUS

Privilege (Book 1)
Prisoner (Book 2)
Book 3 Coming in 2026

Join the mailing list for occasional updates and get a bonus chapter of Privilege! www.meganwobus.com

The Rights to freedom of expression, movement, work, assembly, participation in public affairs, and privacy are hereby limited. These Rights shall not be guaranteed, but earned as Privileges through Certification and a Commitment to the Common Oath.

— Citizen Privileges of the Peaceful Society, 2026

1

AMITY

BALTIMORE, MARYLAND 2034

"AMITY BLOOME!" my mother shouts urgently from the bottom of the stairs of our Baltimore rowhouse. I crack my eyes open. The morning sunlight is streaming through the window of my tiny bedroom, squished in the middle of the upstairs.

"Hang on, I'm almost done," I call and take a deep breath, trying to settle down into the last minute of my Twenty. It's no use, my thoughts are racing now and the calm, detached feeling is slipping away.

When my timer beeps I shut it off and stumble down the hall to the pale, tiled bathroom still in my pajamas. I'm wearing a soft, worn T-shirt I adopted from my dad, and loose shorts.

I hear steps on the stairs. She must be coming up to check on me. There's a loud knock on the door.

"How's it going, Amity? Do you need anything?" I tug

the door open and reveal my mother's narrow, tan face staring back at me. She is tall and pretty, in a way that blends with the power she exudes, her natural command.

She has sharp cheekbones, full lips, and blue eyes like my own, with long brown hair in a braid down her back. The only differences between us are the streaks of gray around her temples and the wrinkles that tighten the corners of her eyes and deepen her smile.

If you can get a smile out of Calista Bloome, you're doing exceptionally well.

I haven't answered her questions but she already has more. "You did your Twenty?" she checks.

"Of course." I haven't needed a reminder to do my required morning meditation for years. She's anxious.

"You need to be out the door by eight," she reminds me sharply, turning on her heel. "In your school uniform," she tosses back from down the hall.

I could stretch it to 8:15 and still get to the courthouse on time but I don't argue, just shove my toothbrush back in the holder and listen to her stepping briskly back downstairs, the quick staccato of her shoes on the wooden steps.

Today is a huge day for me. Thinking back to what the speaker said at graduation yesterday has my heart pumping with anticipation.

"City College High School, class of 2034, tomorrow you have the opportunity to take your Oath and make your commitment to the Peaceful Society of Greater Maryland." The speaker was smiling but her eyes were wide open and grave. "It's a privilege many of our mothers and grandmothers never had a chance to enjoy.

"We have many reasons to be thankful. All of us owe our lives and safety to the sacrifices our mothers and the martyrs of the Peaceful Society made for us. I sincerely encourage each one of you," her eyes flicked around the room, slowing on the groups of young men sitting in the audience, "to fully embrace the opportunities we offer every Citizen regardless of race, creed, or gender." She said the last word with a straight face but there was a low hum from the boys in the room.

Another reason I'm in a hurry. Zeph. He sat next to me in the crowded auditorium, his pale skin and red hair as familiar as my own brown locks. Ever since the Integration, when everything changed, he's lived around the corner, always knocked on my door or I've knocked on his.

I was ten when the war happened and everything changed; a lot of my friends moved away. But that was when Zeph moved in around the corner. After the Integration we explored the streets, safe with security stations sprouting on every block like the newly planted trees, ready to call a Security Officer within minutes any time, night or day.

Zeph and I were both children of women who fought in the Integration and stayed to build the Peaceful Society. The safety of the streets, each inch of city monitored and safeguarded, made our mothers giddy with the freedom they indulgently pushed on us. The Privilege of safety, provided by the Peaceful Society.

"Go, go anywhere," my mother would encourage me. "You can explore all of Baltimore, Amity, the whole city is safe. The whole city is yours."

I buzz around my tiny bedroom, pulling on my uniform

and grabbing what I need to take to the courthouse. The walls are pale blue and my bed is narrow against the wall. I yank the blanket up and straighten the pillow. It's uncommonly neat in here since I might be leaving, tomorrow even, after I've made my Oath.

It's quiet downstairs. My little brother Ethan is already at school. My dad greets me with a wide grin. He's eating eggs and toast before he leaves for his job at the WPA, the Works Progress Administration, that employs most of the men in our neighborhood.

I wiggle my feet into sneakers as my mom flits about, fretting. She must have delayed going to work to make sure I got off okay. It's silly we can't go together, since she works at the courthouse, but the rules are I go to Oath Day without a parent or guardian.

There can be no hint that taking the Oath and committing myself fully to the Peaceful Society is anything other than my own decision. It's also why we can't take the Oath until we graduate from high school.

"Bye, Dad," I call into the house and my mom follows me onto the porch.

"Are you still planning to sign up for HighClear?" she asks, checking for the hundredth time.

"Yes, absolutely," I assure her. Her face relaxes and she nods, giving me a tiny shove.

"Go ahead, Amity. Go in peace." She dismisses me with a hint of her rare smile, ducking back inside.

I turn the familiar corner and Zeph is already waiting in front of his house, backpack on. I hesitate. No matter how many times we've talked about it, no matter how much I've begged him, he claims he's going to refuse the Oath.

He was still talking about it yesterday after graduation. Going on in a whispered hush about a men's colony in Alaska, with runaway men from the Peaceful Society and other territories who are trying to revive the old ways.

A dream or a rumor. I can't imagine there's anything that organized in Alaska all these years after the Integration. I wish he wouldn't talk to me about it; I don't want either of us to get in trouble.

I sympathize with the men who say they are treated as second-class citizens, punished for the violence of their fathers and grandfathers. I want things to change for them, but that change will happen from *inside* the Society, not from a bunch of feral men in Alaska. He should know why we take baby steps in granting the Privileges to men—we took the same history classes.

Zeph nods to me as he takes off down the sidewalk. I try to keep up with his long strides. He taps a light rhythm on his leg as he walks.

"Are you ready for Oath Day?" he asks me, polite and formal.

"Shut up, Zeph. Are you taking the Oath?" I hiss, the reserve I sometimes wear as the daughter of an Officer dropping away. I loop my arm through his, pleading. "Come on. It's time to settle down." My words are a command, a suggestion, and a plea.

Zeph's expression is stubborn and resentful. "You don't understand what it's like."

"What does Miro say? Does he know?" I continue to press. Zeph's boyfriend, Miro, took the Oath last year and he's doing fine. Works for the WPA.

"Miro is doing his own thing," is all Zeph says.

5

I glance at my friend and his lips are pressed in a thin line. Is there anything I can do to convince him that it's better to go ahead and take the Oath? It's not so bad, living as a Citizen. He could try for Clearance, although it's hard to get for men, since the training is so rigorous.

Zeph shakes his head with a sigh. "I'm done talking about it," he grumbles, sidestepping another argument.

I walk quickly, keeping up with him on the last block to the bus stop for our little corner of Northeast Baltimore. I think I'm in shock. He really is planning to refuse the Oath.

In school they say it runs in families: rebelliousness, defiance, and aggression. Maybe that's true because Zeph's father is either an Oath Refuser or an Oath Breaker.

Probably an Oath Breaker. I've never asked. The way he shuffles around their house, thick monitor on his ankle, obviously on a cocktail of meds to curb his aggression, makes me think he broke the Oath and committed violence. We don't talk about his dad.

Not all Oath Refusers are rebellious—some people refuse the Oath for religious reasons, but they're not allowed to hold jobs or have any of the Privileges of being a Citizen. I can't imagine that life for Zeph.

We stand apart from the cluster of people waiting at the bus stop. Electric cars slide by on the street but there's no sign of the bus yet. I glance at the SafeGuard on my wrist for the time. I'll be turning it in for a Citizen SafeGuard after I take the Oath, according to my mom.

We still have plenty of time to get downtown to the courthouse, and the line to get in will be so long it won't even matter if we're punctual. Not that I would ever say that to my mom.

"So what? You're just going to sit at home with your dad?" I can't stop myself from pushing him on this, but I keep my voice whisper soft, not wanting anyone to hear.

Zeph shudders. "No. No way. I have a plan."

Alaska? I mouth silently, rolling my eyes.

There's a pause. His foot taps on the sidewalk. We're standing in front of a wide bench. The bright sun shines on the wooden slats. If you look carefully you can see the shadow of the words that were engraved into benches all around the city: The Greatest City in America.

When my mom was a kid people laughed at the slogan, she told me. It was a time when nearly any adult could own and carry weapons designed to kill other people, just because they felt like it. There were shootings every day in the city. When my mom was growing up in Baltimore, that's the world she lived in.

I was lucky to be born at the same time my mom and grandmother and the other early leaders were forming Mothers Against Violence. The MAV network was able to change many of the gun laws and regulations in the United States.

I was only in first grade when the 2nd Amendment was revoked, but I remember the parties. Everyone was celebrating, honking, banging pots and pans on their porches. MAV only got stronger after that.

It's a privilege to live in Baltimore now in the Peaceful Society of Greater Maryland. It's safe, it's clean, it's a perfect city. Trees line the boulevards and are tucked into the tree pits dug into every available corner of the narrow streets.

Wide gardens fill the parks that replaced the torn-down blocks, tended by the gentle men of the Works Progress Administration. Mom's proud to still live in the house she grew up in, even with surveillance being so much stricter in the city than it is out in the towns. It's worth it for her.

I snap back to the bus stop and Oath Day as Zeph speaks.

"I made contact with a rebel group," he murmurs finally. "You can't tell a soul."

He can't ask me to promise that. He *shouldn't* ask me to promise that, knowing what I'm planning to do at the courthouse today.

"They need people like me." Zeph has always been amazing at programming and tinkering with technology. I'm sure the rebels would be thrilled to have him. "I'm meeting someone there," he continues in an undertone.

"At the courthouse?" Not possible. How would the rebels infiltrate the courthouse, one of the most secure buildings in the city, on Oath Day of all days?

He chances a nod, glancing nervously to the Security Station next to the bus stop, a pole with a camera, microphones, and a blue, glowing button to call for help.

I see it too and erase all worry and concern from my face.

The electric bus pulls up quietly. The squeal of brakes and murmurs of conversation are the only sounds. We hop on and I check the time again as we head down the aisle. It's only a little after 8:40 and we're on track to get to the courthouse by 9:00. I'm not sure if that's enough time to change his mind.

2

AMITY

As Zeph and I sit together on the bus, like we have so many times over the years, he stares out the window and I glance around. This route goes downtown and it's a mix of people heading to jobs and a few kids our age heading to the courthouse, same as we are. The CSOs, Community Security Officers, are in the back.

Each Officer is a different height, her face unique, but all with the same strong build, dressed head to toe in identical white uniforms with their hair pulled into long braids down their backs. Each carries a Taser at her waist and stun baton on her back.

I know the uniform well. My whole life, I've watched my mother put on that same uniform day in and day out. I fully intend to follow her into the Force. There's no greater legacy, no greater service you can give back, than keeping the peace. "Peace is a Privilege" my mom always reminds me, and I believe her.

"Zeph," I say carefully. There are cameras and microphones scattered over the ceiling of the bus.

"You know my grandmother died at Tel Nof." I add the word *please*, forming it silently. Whatever he is planning, I don't want to see him under arrest, a thick monitor on his ankle, all doped up to become a person I don't recognize anymore. I imagine him slumped on the couch next to his father, watching government videos, and I shudder.

"My grandfather also died in the Integration," he says, his brows drawing together.

I didn't know that. Did his grandfather fight for or against the Peaceful Society?

"They sacrificed for us, Zeph," I murmur. Not only the millions of lives lost. The destruction of weapons factories, the haze when the drug fields burned, the new restrictions and rules. The cost was so steep.

Even now, the world population has been shrinking steadily since the invention of the fertility chip. Reproduction was one of the Freedoms we gave up for peace. In our territory it's a Privilege now, only available to Citizens, and must be earned along with the Privileges of Speech, Movement, Work, Assembly, Privacy, and Participation in Public Affairs.

"You make your choices, I make mine," Zeph says. He likes to argue about free will with me, likes to tell me all about how men should have more control over their own lives.

My dad has plenty of control over his life. He works for the WPA, like most men who are Citizens. He took the Oath and as long as he wears his SafeGuard and checks in for

Citizen Training once a year, he's given equal Privileges with women. In theory, he could undergo training to try for Clearance. Then he could hold a better-paying job, a Position of Power, even if only a fraction of men make it through.

Clearance training is more rigorous than training for Citizens, and HighClear, the training to become a Security Officer, is the toughest of all. It requires absolute self-control and nonaggression, total nonreactivity of speech, thought, and movement. Few men even volunteer to try it.

The buildings outside the bus window grow larger and look scrubbed, the marble shining. Even the concrete appears immaculately clean in this area of the city that houses the central CSO station, the courthouse, and nearby government buildings.

At the bus stop I stand, tugging Zeph behind me until we're out on the street. We watch the heavier traffic in this area for a minute, e-cars backing up at the stoplight in front of the bus stop.

I turn to him, fearful. Tension spreads throughout my body, my chest rising and falling rapidly despite my efforts to slow my breathing down.

"What will happen?" I ask quietly as we stand together. I clutch his hand in my own sweaty palm, not ready to move toward the courthouse yet. The building behind us is the Central Security Station. Women in white walk briskly on the sidewalk and hurry up the steps to work. Zeph glances around nervously.

"I'll leave," he says simply, and I know what he's talking about. It's his crazy plan to get to Anchorage, to a rebel militia there. "Or go underground."

I glance down at the pale concrete beneath our feet.

Kids whisper in school about men's rights groups meeting underground, in the old subway tunnels. Fighting with each other more than getting organized from the sound of it, their capacity diminished but not entirely extinguished.

"You could refuse the Oath also, Amity, you don't have to stay here," he says in a mournful voice. I heave a deep sigh. He knows I've made up my mind, the same as him.

I've known I was going to train for HighClear since I was a little girl, dressing up in all my white clothes and borrowing my mother's weapons belt. Her empty weapons belt, that is. There's no way she'd let me touch her Taser.

He sees the answer in my eyes.

"Yeah," he mutters. Pain flashes over his face. The hug he draws me into is sad, defeated. In other words, it's goodbye.

"You're my best friend, Amity," he says into my hair.

A tear slips down my cheek. If that's true, why is he going to refuse the Oath? Or whatever he's planning?

"Go in Peace," I tell him as goodbye. We'll walk together down the block to the courthouse, but I don't want to say goodbye there, in a long line with the other kids ready to take their Oaths. I'll say it now, because once I'm there I'll be Amity Bloome, my mother's daughter, granddaughter of Selene Bloome, martyr of the Integration.

As I expected, the line into the courthouse is long, snaking down and around the block. Zeph and I walk along the row of teenagers, laughing and joking, many of them sleepy after a night of post-graduation partying.

I greet a couple of friends from the swim team, mostly

serious girls like me who are going up for Clearance. You need high grades to be considered, and those don't come without a lot of work. I never had time to date or socialize much in high school.

If the Peaceful Society accepts me into HighClear, I'll only have tonight with my family to say goodbye and get ready and then I'll be sent off to the Institute with the other girls.

The thought of leaving my little bedroom, my parents, and my brother Ethan, opens a crack in my heart.

I imagine the barracks: cold, white and bare. Security Officers don't indulge. When my mom is home she does all these little things, taking a warm bath, drinking a cup of tea, even cuddling under a thick blanket on the couch, and calls them her luxuries.

I think luxury would be having the latest e-car or living in one of the huge houses up on the hill.

Zeph walks in front of me, and it's not his usual carefree stride. Each step is deliberate, and I see his eyes scan up and down the line.

We finally get to the end and begin the wait. Luckily the line is moving at a quick shuffle. I assume they're scanning everyone's SafeGuard. Maybe there are even metal detectors. I remember them from when I was a kid.

During the Integration, metal detectors were literally everywhere. There would even be checkpoints on the sidewalk with CSOs monitoring the foot traffic. They were catching each and every gun for the buyback, and enforcing the new, weak peace.

I'm excited to maybe walk through one. I don't know what weapons anyone would dare bring to the courthouse.

There are Officers stationed all over the place. I guess it could detect if you had a knife. I assume Zeph has thought of all that.

Our eyes meet but I can't tell what he's thinking. All these years, hanging out, watching our siblings, walking to school day in and day out, and I still wonder if Zeph is trying to smuggle a knife into the courthouse.

What would be the point anyway—you'd only get in trouble.

Inside the wide marble lobby, gray plastic boxes line up like doorways with teenagers waiting to walk through. On the other side, guards with handheld scanners scan each kid's SafeGuard.

Zeph goes first, then I walk through the metal detector. Nothing happens. There's a girl scanning a couple of kids in the uniform of a rival school. A different guard steps around her and comes over to us to bend over Zeph's wrist.

This guard is a man, dressed like the other guards in white against his deep brown skin, his shoulders broad and wide, a head taller than the women scanning wrists around him.

It's so curious to see a man working as a guard. He must have Clearance to be allowed to scan SafeGuards. Is he support staff? I gaze around the room and everyone is getting their wrists scanned, then moving down the hall in clusters.

No one is staring at this guard. No one except me. His hair is tight black curls, clipped close to his head. He's still bending over Zeph's wrist, getting the scanner to work. He must be older than me if he's a courthouse guard but he doesn't seem very old. More like a bigger, stronger version of the boys I went to school with.

The guard's gaze rises to meet mine and my stomach drops. I know those eyes, dark brown, nearly black. There's no mistaking his starkly handsome, strong features with dark brows above a smooth, brown jawline.

He may not be in fourth grade anymore, but the tall, serious boy I used to see at my mother's MAV meetings stares directly back, standing behind Zeph, as if he can feel my focus on him. He's the son of my mom's friend Mikayla, but I never saw them again after the Integration.

The guard starts slightly. It's almost imperceptible except that I'm obsessively staring at him, trying to remember his name. After a brief glance at my school uniform he bends back over Zeph's wrist, but I think I see a shadow of a smile, and maybe confusion as well.

My eyes fall to his hands and narrow. What is taking so long? Is the scanner broken?

I catch an unexpected flicker of movement, the guard sending what looks like a SafeGuard up into the sleeve of his white uniform while Zeph flexes his wrist, wrapped in an identical SafeGuard. Did they just switch them? I don't know how you could do that with a scanner. There's a tool the doctor uses to fit a new one on me at my checkup.

My heart races as Zeph takes a few steps and Mikayla's son looks up, meeting my eyes, waiting for me to step forward.

3

AMITY

I TRY NOT to get distracted as he looms over me, his hand engulfing my wrist as he holds up my SafeGuard to scan. He smells like pine soap and something faintly familiar, chlorine or some other chemical they use in the pool at school.

"What are you doing here?" I demand. "And what did you do to his SafeGuard?" I speak through clenched lips and teeth. I see it, a nervous flick of the guard's eyes to Zeph before his face smooths over.

"Nothing to worry about," he murmurs in a low rumble while he holds the scanner over my wrist, but his brow furrows. His hand is warm and dry, the fingers long with no jewelry or hint of markings on his smooth skin. Our arms contrast: my tan skin dusted with freckles is pale beside his strong, brown forearm.

"That's my friend," I whisper. "What did you do to him?"

He stares at me for a beat. "Calm down, Pepper."

I jerk in response. It *is* him! The other kids at the MAV meetings used to call me Pepper, because of my freckles.

"Your mom is Mikayla Adamson," I hiss. "What are you doing here? How are you a guard?"

I think this kid is eighteen, just like me. He doesn't answer but finishes the scan, still holding on to my wrist like he's reluctant to let go. I leave my arm there, sitting in his warm grasp.

"I don't know what you're talking about," he says to me in a low voice.

"Liar," I snap, pulling my wrist away.

There's a huff from Zeph in front of me and Mikayla's son gives a shake, as if clearing his head, and takes a step back. He doesn't call to the graduates waiting behind me, just turns slowly to watch us as we leave.

Is he watching Zeph? Or is he watching me?

We join a group heading down the hall to the wide staircase. I don't want to look back, but I can't help taking a peek. The guard is scanning another girl's SafeGuard now, her wrist limp in his hand, but his eyes are not on her. This time there's no doubt—his gaze is bound to me. I keep searching my memory, trying to remember more about him. He was a quiet kid who kept to himself, but there was a time I knew his name. It was something short.

With my heart refusing to slow down, I turn and will myself to face forward as my thoughts rush in all directions. I glance over at Zeph and his wrist, but his SafeGuard looks identical to mine.

Here I am, walking with Zeph. If he does something stupid, will I get in trouble, too? Could this hurt my chances of becoming a Security Officer?

My stomach, already on edge at the prospect of taking the Oath and Zeph's foolish plans, dips again as I imagine myself being blamed, imagine my mother getting in trouble with the Peaceful Society.

I try to swallow and my mouth is dry as sand. What am I going to do?

At the top of the stairs the flow of people splits apart, as everyone files into wide doors on either side of the hallway. Both sides are courtrooms. I see rows of wooden benches and marble on the walls and ceiling. I pull to the right, ready to enter, but Zeph tries to slip off to the other room.

"Oh, no you don't," I hiss, following him as closely as I can across the hall to the courtroom on the left.

"Amity, can you just go?" he says, motioning with his eyes across the hall.

"Zeph, I swear," I say under my breath, my temper rising. We've stopped and there's a pile-up behind us while we argue.

"Keep it moving," a guard's high, bored voice calls and the decision is made. We're entering together and filing with the rest of the line into a row between long wooden benches.

In the front of the room there's a fenced-off area with a group of desks. In one corner is a flag of the Peaceful Society, a stylized dove holding a twig from the olive tree. On the other side is a flag of the United Nations.

I sit with Zeph next to me, and he's way too still for my comfort. We've been friends long enough for me to know that he's always in motion, foot tapping, looking around, leg jiggling. If he has something in his hands he's either taking it apart or putting it back together.

Right now he's sitting entirely still and it's scaring me. I let my hand creep over to his wrist, trying to feel his SafeGuard, but he jerks away.

"Not now, Amity," he murmurs. I glance around. Everywhere there are teenagers talking, laughing, some of them rowdy on the other side of the room.

"Come on," I say quietly.

"No." His voice is low, final. "It's done."

"What do you mean it's done? And who was that, I..." I hesitate, not sure whether to admit I recognized the guard.

"Stop it." Zeph's voice is tight.

I turn away. My heart, beating against my chest, has not slowed down. I wonder if I'm having a panic attack.

A bunch of adults file through a door in the front. The Guardian for Baltimore and her assistant set up at the desk in the middle. A couple of CSOs sit off to the right, and a group of guards from the lobby file in and cluster in the back. He's there, the guard who scanned me.

It's impossible not to notice him. The little kid who would wander off into the woods behind the community center where our MAV group met is *very* grown up and *very* handsome. He could be modeling for advertisements or starring in government videos, even in his simple white shirt and uniform pants.

His face is carefully blank and he's staring at the wall, not at us, but I think he knows we're here, and he's keeping tabs on us. There's something in his posture, how he shifts a bit when my gaze returns to him. I'm not sure how he's doing it, but he's watching us.

The Guardian calls the room to order.

"This is the day you join the movement to eradicate violence and live in a peaceful, safe, and unified Society."

I'm listening to her, but I'm watching Mikayla's son. There's not a flicker of reaction on his face as she speaks. She talks about taking the Oath, what will happen if we apply for Clearance or HighClear, and what will happen if we refuse the Oath.

"A commitment to the Common Oath grants you the Privileges of Citizenship in the Peaceful Society," she says. Then she quotes the Universal Accord we all learned in school.

"Rights shall not be guaranteed, but earned as Privileges through Certification and a Commitment to the Common Oath."

We've all been through Citizen training in school, training for years in nonviolent speech and action, de-escalation, emotional regulation, and conflict resolution. All that's left for us to become full Citizens is to take the Oath.

The process starts and people are called up one by one. The assistant confers quietly with each new person who enters the little gate and approaches her desk. Then they move to stand before the Guardian, raising their right hand to take the Oath.

Some get directed to the desk on the right, and the Officers take the information of the girls I assume are going up for Clearance. Groups of young women and men file back out the doors we came in, required to make one more stop to get their new SafeGuard on the way out.

Then one boy has a longer conversation with the assistant. He shakes his head, and they talk more. Sweat slides down the side of his forehead. There's a slight tremor in his hands.

The woman turns and nods to the guards behind her. One of them steps forward and walks with the boy to a door on the left, and they leave without taking the Oath.

Zeph tightens next to me and my eyes flick not to him but back to the guard, the boy I knew from before, standing in uniform. He's turned toward us now where we're sitting. His eyes return my gaze coolly, flicking between Zeph and me. I'm sure worry is written all over my face but he doesn't respond, only glances away, his face blank.

After another span of Oath Takers, another boy refuses the Oath and leaves to the left with a guard.

They get to our school, working their way through the kids in my class until the assistant calls Zeph's name. I squeeze his hand once, then he pulls it away, walking with slow carefulness to the front of the room. Zeph dips his head down, having the longer conversation that I've dreaded.

Like the others, the assistant calls for a guard over her shoulder. My ears ring as the guard I recognize steps forward. He makes eye contact with me, this time with warning in his eyes. He walks casually to Zeph's side and they turn together, heading to the left.

A cry, a warning, forms in my throat but I swallow it down. I'm being called up right now, right after Zeph, to take my Oath.

I have to wrench my gaze away from the door swinging shut at the side of the courtroom as I push through the gate.

There's an easy smile on the assistant's face, and the

Security Officers nod to me in recognition of Calista Bloome's daughter. I quickly confirm I'm going to take the Oath and want to be considered for HighClear training.

With my right hand raised next to my shoulder, I read aloud the words of the Oath.

I am a citizen of the Peaceful Society
I reject violence in all forms
My freedom is a Privilege
My legacy is peace

My voice shakes on the last line as the words sink into me. Everything I fear flashes before my eyes: Zeph committing violence, getting put on probation, drugged and monitored. Or worse, Zeph and the guard committing an attack, people getting hurt or even killed.

The only person here who knows what just happened is me.

I stand, frozen, while the Guardian cocks her head, waiting patiently.

My legacy is peace, I just swore in the Oath. But right now my legacy is not peace. It's deception, keeping this all a secret when people's safety and lives could be put at risk by my silence. My grandmother didn't die for me to cover up for a bunch of rebels, no matter how old our friendship.

"Amity?" she asks curiously, while I stand there, stuck.

"Zeph," I say, my voice cracking, low. "And the guard. Rebels."

Her attention sharpens and she leans forward slightly.

"He switched," I stumble over the words, "he switched his SafeGuard."

23

Now she motions to the seated Officers. They instantly register her concern and stand, their chairs scraping the floor in unison.

The CSOs listen intently as she speaks to them in a low voice. I catch a few words before they move smoothly toward the door on the left, speaking into their SafeGuards, pulling batons off their backs.

There's no shouting, no noise, only soft commands as the white-clad Officers check the corridor, then move out into the hall.

I'm still standing in front of the Guardian, shocked and worried, my heart refusing to slow down. Then she stands and addresses the room.

"There will be a ten-minute break and then we will resume."

It's so quiet you could hear a pin drop. No one responds to the announcement.

"Amity Bloome," she says, turning. "You'd better come with me."

JANUARY 9, 2016

My heart breaks at the final number of murders in Baltimore in 2015 ("Deadliest year in Baltimore history ends with 344 homicides"). The numbers only tell a small piece of the story. Every man, woman, and child killed in our city—twenty-two of the deaths were children—leaves a hole in the lives of their parents, children, relatives, and friends.

I think of one example from my own life. My mother went through a deep depression after the death of her mother. She had trouble eating and taking a shower, getting out of bed, and getting through the day without crying. We should not leave the living to grieve alone.

Several local mothers and I recently formed a Baltimore chapter of Mothers Against Violence, a new organization with an old mission. Mothers in our city have always provided comfort to our children, nieces and nephews, friends and loved ones. We refuse to ignore the pain and suffering that shootings and murders cause in our city.

Mothers Against Violence, or MAV, offers comfort, therapy, meals, and financial support to all victims of gun violence. Whether a shooting has affected your physical, emotional, or spiritual health or that of your loved ones, let us know how we can support you.

By refusing to sweep these deaths under the rug, and focusing on healing and remembering those who were killed, we will change our city. The reaction to a murder should not be a vow to avenge the death with more violence, but a supported journey from grief and coping to acceptance and peace.

We ask everyone in Baltimore: please think about what you may have done, consciously or unconsciously, to contribute to violence in our city. None of us are wholly innocent, but all of us have the opportunity to do better in 2016.

Please join us at a MAV meeting soon. All are welcome. Find our schedule at mav.org.

Sincerely,
Mikayla Adamson
Homewood, Baltimore

4

VALE

THE ROADS in Baltimore are so smooth. It's like the
pavement is as soft as the people down here. I ride in the
passenger seat of a large WPA van. When I turn around, I
see a group of men sitting in the back of the van on padded
benches through a glass pane. There are seatbelts back
there.

I snort and turn back to the driver. "Don't speed."

He taps the brake as we crawl back to a painful thirty
mph. We have two more men to pick up before heading out
of the city. We won't be able to use this WPA van many
more times before we switch things up. I'll miss it. It's way
more comfortable than the network of tunnels and smelly
garbage scows we were using before this.

The streets of Baltimore are swarming with people this
morning. School is out for the summer so parents and kids
are on their way to parks and camps. Every block I see the
ubiquitous security stations of the Peaceful Society, ready
to bring a swarm of PS soldiers at the slightest infraction.

We tinted the windows of this van a little bit, just enough to disrupt the facial recognition technology, but not enough to draw the attention of the soldiers. There are WPA vans everywhere, filled with men mostly, heading to work sites and parks. We blend right in.

I turn and press a button to project my voice into the back.

"Make sure you change into the uniforms before we get to the checkpoint," I growl. They'd better get on that. If we get caught at the checkpoint on the way out of town we'll all be sent to Frederick and shot full of drugs before I can even get a message to the Forge.

I focus on my breathing while intrusive thoughts about Amity Bloome keep disturbing me. Oddly, she's a friend of our recruit. The last time I saw her she was a scrawny fourth grader, playing tag and bossing her little brother around, covered in freckles with wide blue eyes.

Now she's tall, and stunning, and she wasn't afraid of me, only confused to see me and worried about her friend. I wonder if I'll ever see her again. She didn't seem like typical PS, only fit to live a soft, padded life within the checkpoints of their little paradise.

I've known my whole life how Greater Maryland is a failed state, how they made up their own religion and ran rampant with it across Maryland and beyond, DC and Philly too, forcing everyone to take their Oath. Performing their sick punishments on anyone who breaks it.

My father's bitter words come back to me. "They will do anything to feel safe. They didn't care about your mom, Vale, they sent her off to Natanz knowing it was a death sentence. They think they can change us, drug us, brainwash out the aggression. It's not our nature. We were meant to run free, to fight and protect and take back what's ours."

That's my father for you. He means what he says. My upbringing, once we left Baltimore, was big on training and fighting. I've still got scars from what I went through with him. Send Vale to train, get the doctor to fix Vale up. Rinse and repeat.

I should forget about Amity along with everything else in this evil city. I'm sure she stood there and took her Oath, ready to go deeper into the sick web of women exacting their revenge on a world they hate and a reality they refuse to accept.

I crack my knuckles, and the feel of her wrist in my hand flashes back to me. The wild part inside me, that natural part of being human they talk about back at the Forge, roars at the memory of her skin and the flash of her blue eyes.

I don't want to destroy her, no matter how many times I've been told that's what we must do to the PS. I want something different. I want to protect her, to feel her in my arms.

It must be a messed-up reaction to what people are like down here, like lambs to the slaughter, at least the ones who aren't soldiers. It's like no one's ever told them the facts of life: we live, we fight, and we die.

There's no point to all this nonsense: the security, the smooth, perfect roads and the clean, sanitized sidewalks. All the nonviolence training in the world won't change the truth. Life is short and you die, and you take none of your pretty things with you.

I prefer it up north where we don't pretend. It's not a problem when a man gets angry, it's just human nature. It doesn't mean things have gone wrong and we need to medicate him. It's a natural feeling in a natural body and nothing else.

The van stops and one of my father's undercover lieutenants appears on the sidewalk with two worried-looking men—boys really—behind him. This time of year is crazy for us.

Making all the kids take the Oath at the same time separates the boys from the men who don't want to lie down and take orders from women, build their gardens and plant their trees for the rest of their lives. That means more recruits for us.

"The uniforms are in the side locker," I remind them through the speaker. "When we stop at the checkpoint, we are members of the WPA heading to a worksite near Morgantown, West Virginia. You expect to be gone several weeks. You are all Citizens. Any questions?"

None come. These guys are scared, and that's fair. But I do this a lot and the chances are pretty good we get through and this all works out. If it doesn't, be scared then. But they've been raised here, and it's going to be a long road for them to become the kind of men who survive the Forge, who can make it up north. Alaska is not for the weak.

That was our last stop but we drive for a little longer on the streets, staying under the speed limit. We're not waiting for any particular signal to head toward the checkpoint out of the city. As the ranking officer here, it's up to me and my instinct for when the time is right.

"Turn here, let's get on the highway," I tell the driver.

He nods and we head carefully onto the ramp, gathering speed and heading up and out of the city. There are not a lot of cars on the road. Vehicles are heavily regulated, like everything else down here: dangerous, polluting, blah, blah, blah.

When we get to the last exit before the checkpoint I have the driver pull over for a minute. I walk around the back and pull the door open. The guys are in their uniforms. They seem fine except for the scared faces.

"Hey," I snap. "Smile a little, relax your shoulders. You're going to work. It's going to be boring." They paint their faces with tense smiles and slump slightly. It's not perfect, but it's better.

"Grab some tools," I direct them, and each man reaches for a shovel or bucket and one carefully balances the Weedwhacker on his lap. That looks better.

We're ready. I take the driver's seat this time. If we're lucky, I'll talk us through the checkpoint. Even if they search the van, they won't find anything amiss unless they deep scan our SafeGuards. That could get dicey. I'm not going to give them any reason to do that.

I start up the engine and pull back onto the highway, only to slow my speed for the checkpoint that's a mile up ahead. A large metal apparatus hangs over the road and takes pictures of the van as I drive under it, registering our speed, license plate, scanning for weapons, not that they'll find anything.

We should be in the clear. Everything has been arranged in the PS system for this "work trip" and there will be someone bringing the van back with workers, keeping the whole mission seeming legitimate.

I slow down further as soldiers, women in white, stand along the road, watching the vehicles in line, their braids hanging down their backs. Will Amity Bloome enter training to become one of them? The "CSOs" as they call them?

Or will she sit behind a desk somewhere, married to some dumb, harmless man, sheltered in a suffocating PS city? I remember the flash of her eyes and her sharp questions.

She could be more than that. I can see her holding her own up north. She's wasted here. But there's nothing to be done about it. Why am I even thinking about her again? I shake my head and shoulders as I try to throw off the nagging feeling, the connection I felt to her. I've got eleven men to keep safe and get through this checkpoint right now.

I roll down the window as I bring the van to a slow, gentle stop next to a small security booth. I've also changed into a WPA uniform. It's a normal, everyday work trip. We're over the moon excited to plant tulip bulbs in Morgantown.

"Hi there." A woman stares at me from the booth. She smiles, though not with her eyes.

"Hello." I'm friendly, but don't offer anything. Let her be in charge of the interaction.

"What's your name and where are you headed?" she says approvingly. These women are so predictable. They love it when you submit to them.

I give the fake name I've been assigned and describe the

work trip we're taking. The soldier nods as she listens. She holds out a scanner and I present my wrist for her to scan my SafeGuard.

This is where everything could go sideways. Things should be in order with my fake identity, but we only filled in a year or two of back information, so if she scrolls too far she'll run into a blank slate. As her finger flicks and flicks I hold my breath.

Her eyes finally raise to mine but they are bored, unimpressed. That means they did a great job with the fake identity. I want to tell her who I am just to get her reaction, but I keep my expression dull, my eyes down.

"We'll just have to take a look in the back. Twelve of you in all?" she asks.

"Yup." I leave it there. I don't know why she needs to check the van. Maybe it's a new thing.

"We have a record of a couple of stops you made," she says, checking a tablet.

"Yeah," I hesitate. "Just getting the crew together." She doesn't answer, just steps out of her booth, bringing her scanner and coming around to the passenger side of the van. She scans Mark, a grunt from the Forge, and skims his bio before giving him a curt nod and shutting the passenger door, but not before her eyes sweep the interior. These guys better follow my instructions and stay quiet and still.

Breathe, relax, you're heading on a work trip, I coach myself. I'm sweating, but I'm able to keep my breathing slow and relaxed, and my heart rate mostly cooperates. The gravel crunches as the woman walks around to the back. A soldier with a stun baton strapped to her back steps out to join her. Maybe they don't look in the back of unfamiliar vehicles alone.

The two of them sigh about a meeting they have to attend at lunch and talk about plans for later. Then I hear the sound of the handle and the door to the back of the van squeaking as they pull it open.

5

VALE

AT FIRST THERE'S only the quiet murmur of voices. I glance over at Mark, but he shrugs. He's sweating and his face looks a little shiny.

"Should we go back there?" he asks in a low voice.

My eyes flick to the road, the signage, and the guard booth while I think.

"Hang on a minute," I tell him.

So we sit, and it's hotter now in the late morning. The sun is strong. I can feel it through the windshield. The air inside the front of the van is starting to get a little stifling.

We're so close to the border. We're almost out of here. Every time I come down I know there's a chance I could get caught and taken to one of the camps in Western Maryland where they hold men.

The description we got from the last man to come from those camps still lives in my brain, impossible to forget.

The PS emptied the jails after the Integration and pretended everything was solved. But there were still people they didn't want...couldn't stand to have in their perfect little world. Men were stuck in home detention, or put on depo trains and shipped up to New England.

And there were men like me. Men they don't trust, with good reason. From the start they were setting up camps in old state parks in the mountains around Frederick. If a guy did something wrong he might get stuck at home with an ankle monitor. But if he fought back, raised arms against the PS, that was a different punishment. That got you stuck in their "reeducation centers."

The man described all sorts of things a pretty PS girl like Amity Bloome knows nothing about: shackles, deprivation, interrogation, forced medication, and endless hours of therapy and reeducation.

Here's the thing—very few men come out. Are they dying in there? Is the PS shipping them to the Southwest? We don't know of men being let out and back into the PS. A couple of men escaped, mostly guys who had outdoor skills and could pick up the old Appalachian Trail and follow it up and out of Greater Maryland.

"Vale," Mark says under his breath, and I look up, seeing another PS soldier with a face scanner coming out of a building and walking toward the van.

"Alright, let's go" I mutter and open my door, climbing down as Mark follows on his side. I slow my movements down, slump a little. Try to remember I'm a sleepy WPA leader who doesn't want to be late to his call time.

I mosey around the van to where they've pulled one man out. His eyes, dark, are wide and wild. The new soldier holds the face scanner, waiting for it to power up.

"Hi," I say, looking around at the women.

I glance into the van where the men clutch their tools, staring at the floor. I see some knuckles whitening and hope the PS soldiers haven't noticed.

"Hi," the guard from the booth says shortly, flicking on the screen of her SafeGuard. She doesn't seem inclined to tell me what's going on.

"Uuuuh...." I draw it out. "We're supposed to be there tonight."

"I'm sure safety is your top priority," she snaps, still staring at her wrist.

I wait silently.

"Look up," the woman with the face scanner says, and the man raises his head, still looking nervous as hell.

Dude, chill out, I think silently. Our freedom's on the line and this guy is losing it, not looking very dependable.

"We'll have to detain this man, Mr.—" She grabs his wrist to look at his SafeGuard without permission, "Blackwall."

Anger ripples up my spine at their treatment of him, but I let it wash through me and drain away. I can't be influenced by that right now.

"How long will it take?" I ask.

They laugh. It's pretty funny, I guess, sending a man to a detention camp. The soldier with the weapons finally looks me in the face.

"You guys can go," she says, without answering my question. I force my face into confusion.

She slows down like she's talking to a child and points. "*He's* staying here with us," she drawls, "and *you* can drive to your worksite now. Without him."

"He's...he's on the crew," I say stupidly.

She sighs. "I know he's on your crew." She exchanges an eye roll with the other women. "This man is displaying signs of extreme anxiety. He may be a danger to himself or others. We need to detain him for questioning."

Questioning. That doesn't sound good. I make a rough guess about how long until he cracks and tells them everything. Judging from the wild eyes, I'd guess we have ten minutes from when they start grilling him. I can only hope they hold him for a while first.

I do some quick recalculating of the plan while I shrug.

We'll have to leave him. With a submissive nod to the soldiers, I close the doors of the van carefully and move back to the driver's seat.

"Give me one more minute," the guard says to me and walks with the two soldiers leading the man over into a building at the side of the road.

I open the com to the back.

"Everything okay back there?" I ask.

"No," one of them mutters. There's a couple of affirmative grunts.

"Is that it? Is he gonna give us up?" a man asks, and it's Zeph, the guy who was at the courthouse with Amity.

"They'll probably throw him in a holding cell and let us head out," I tell them. "We'll be on our way in a minute."

"What are they going to do to him?" Zeph asks.

"If he stays calm? Maybe deport him. If he mentions the Forge? He'll be put in a detention camp."

Mark squirms in his seat beside me, no doubt aware of how many things can go wrong at this point.

"Everybody breathe." I don't want to scare them, but I feel I have to say it. "If something happens and they take you, hold out as long as you can to let us get some distance from the border." I glance through the glass and there's nervous nodding.

"Yeah," one man says.

The door opens and the PS guard walks slowly back to the road, chatting into her SafeGuard. She doesn't look at all concerned, which is a good sign. She climbs into the booth and gives me a bored wave, not bothering to make eye contact.

Letting a breath out, I start the car and slowly pull away from the curve.

"Okay, we're okay," Mark says softly next to me. He looks in the mirror, watching the checkpoint shrink behind us as I ease us back onto the highway and gather speed as slowly as I can stand.

"Okay," I say into the com, and I hear a rustle and sighs of relief from the back. "We'll be between territories for a couple of hours and I'll let you know when we cross into the Midwest. We'll stop once we're inside."

I glance over at Mark and back to the road. He's unlocking the glove compartment.

A few minutes later he's got his SafeGuard off. Thinking about the man back at the border, I pull off the highway to take back roads. When we stop he gets the SafeGuard off me and all the new recruits.

Their faces, looking at their bare wrists, show wonder and relief. Every single one of them has a pale circle around their wrist where the device has been for the last eight years, replaced with an updated model and bigger size each year.

I see a couple of them shake their wrists, gaze continually drawn back to the empty stretch of skin.

I flex my wrist as well, glad to be free of it. I don't even wear an e-watch at home; I can't stand the feeling of having something strapped to my wrist.

I remember when I got my first SafeGuard, the pride and happiness on my mom's face. Phones were confiscated along with weapons, but the SafeGuard would let her know where I was and let her communicate with me. It would help her keep me safe at all times.

If only they had been as concerned with keeping her safe, she'd still be with me today. The anger rises, crawling up into my chest and my throat.

"Back in the van," I snap at the guys, who look a little confused at my bad mood while they are all grinning at their empty wrists.

I climb in and slam the door.

I do what I can for the Forge, but no matter how many men we get out of the PS, no matter what my father's plans are to retake what is rightfully ours, none of it can do what I want more than anything in the world. None of it will get my mother back.

DECEMBER 15, 2016

It's a sad day to see that Baltimore murders are on track for another record-breaking year ("Murder Ink 12/14/16: 3 murders this week; 299 murders this year"). Despite the news, Mothers Against Violence continues to organize for peace this year in Baltimore and nationwide. We sent support to the victims of mass shootings in Orlando and around the country, and helped the parents, children, and families of victims in our own city.

Through our research, we know that over half of Americans have been affected by gun violence and in Baltimore the percentage is much higher. In Baltimore City, guns kill more children than any other cause of death.

Residents of Baltimore, it's time to take a stand. We need to heal from this trauma, but you can't heal a scab you continue to scratch. Call your congresspeople today and tell them to support the Commonsense Gun Guidelines bill that will require trigger locks on every gun and background checks for every gun purchase.

Violence has affected all of our lives, but we can work to change that for the future. Find out more at MAVBaltimore.com.

Sincerely,
Mikayla Adamson
Mothers Against Violence

6

AMITY

My heart is pounding. Every thump feels like it's going to cause damage inside me.

I recognize the feelings of anxiety and panic and run through my training. This is exactly the kind of emotional state that must be controlled in order to act rationally, calmly, and with restraint.

I stare at the back of the Guardian as I follow her. She's tall like me and wearing white like a CSO with a long brown and silver braid hanging down her back. To the rhythm of my thumping heart, we walk to the door in the back of the courtroom and down the hall. It's so quiet even our soft footsteps echo. I wonder if they can hear them inside the courtroom, see our shadows through the crack under the door after she closes it.

What is going to happen to Zeph? The question vibrates inside me. I don't fear for myself, but I fear for my friend. My poor, delusional friend who has put himself and his family in danger with this nonsense.

The anxiety that he may be hurt or imprisoned because of this—surely he will be—is a heavy stone in my stomach. Could I have done more to convince him? Could I have done something to avoid this?

The lock clicks as the Guardian opens the door to her chambers and it shakes me out of my haze. She gestures toward one of two chairs and goes to sit heavily in the ornate chair behind her desk. She sighs with a wry expression at the overly fancy surroundings. Something tells me she doesn't think any more of the marble and the heavily polished desk than I do.

These are relics of a system of justice that had it completely wrong. They took people who had lost their way, let their negative emotions control them, and imprisoned them in ways that would only worsen their reactions and deepen their trauma.

It was an inhuman way of dealing with things, the revolving door of prison. Violence in the system, violence out of the system, nothing ever changed. No matter how many people they put in jail, they never got rid of the violence in society. Our way is much better.

We sit silently for a moment until there's a soft knock on the door. When the door swings open I get another shock, seeing a familiar set of shoulders and braid and register my mother as she turns to look at me.

There's nothing written on her face. My mother is too well trained to let her emotions dictate her expression, but there's something around her eyes, fear maybe, that tells me the news is not good. She sits down in the chair beside me and starts to speak, but the Guardian also starts at the same time and my mother stops in respect.

"Amity," the Guardian says to me. "How are you feeling?"

How am I feeling? The question swirls, finding nothing to hold on to. But following my training, I start a rapid body scan, naming the feelings I recognize.

"Anxious. Fearful. Worried. Oh, I guess that's the same as anxious, sorry..." I trail off, searching for anything else.

The Guardian gives a curt nod as my mom reaches out to hold my hand. Her fingers are long like mine, smooth and warm, and she gives my hand a squeeze that I gratefully return.

"You are worried about your friend?" the Guardian guesses correctly.

I nod.

"He is unharmed. We let them escape."

I swallow and control my features. My mother has no reaction at all. She knew. But what about the guard, the boy I remember from MAV? Should I say who I think he is?

"We believe they are heading north to Anchorage," the Guardian tells me, relieving me of the responsibility of spilling that information as well. A quick twist of relief in my chest.

"Oh, Zeph." I respond without thinking.

The Guardian nods but cocks her head to the side. Then she takes a deep breath, thinking. I wait.

"This whole situation has given us an opportunity, Amity."

"Prepare yourself," my mother murmurs. It's something she's said to me my whole life right before bad news or an unexpected development. And so out of habit I brace, emotionally.

The Guardian's eyes soften at the unease showing on my face.

"Your first mission for your HighClear training will be to follow Zeph to Alaska. You will be deported undercover and we will arrange for your travel through Canada to Anchorage."

The words sound like a story out of a book.

"We believe the men Zeph left with," my mother tells me, "belong to a men's militia called the Forge. Your job will be to reach out to the Forge, find Zeph, and make a connection to the organization. Collect information that we need."

"Mom." I shake my head. "I just—I literally just took my Oath." I'm eighteen years old. "Wouldn't someone else be better?" I start to argue, like I don't have any training at all. Like a child.

"Amity," my mother interrupts me. "You showed your dedication to the Peaceful Society today and you've earned the trust of our leadership. We need someone like you for this mission, someone with a personal connection to a new recruit. Zeph didn't see you take the Oath. You'll say that you refused the Oath and came to find him."

"I can't." I stop, realizing I'm arguing again and dismissing her.

"I'm not sure he'll believe that," I correct myself. "I was trying to convince him to take it. The Oath." My mother and the Guardian both sharpen their gaze at the admission that I knew what he was planning.

"Did he ask you to leave with him?" my mother asks.

I can't lie to her. "Yes."

"That only helps, Amity. If you were hiding this

before, he'll believe you hid it again." Shame burns my cheeks as the Guardian considers and then nods in agreement.

"We will provide you with clothing," the Guardian tells me. "There will be cash and a phone number sewn inside the pants. Once you're out of Greater Maryland, buy a cell phone and contact us on the number. If possible you should also purchase a weapon."

My eyes grow big at that.

"At least ask about it, seem interested. It's what an Oath Refuser would do," my mom adds.

They stop and wait, presumably for me to ask questions, but I'm frozen. Is this real? I open my mouth to ask about the guard who left with Zeph, the boy I recognized, but the Guardian continues briskly.

"Amity, your mother will take you to change and go over your directions. The Peaceful Society thanks you for your service. You said you were afraid for your friend. We have not hurt him in any way. Maybe you can convince him to come home and take the Oath." She smiles wryly. "We're not interested in fighting the militias in Anchorage, but we must keep our citizens safe from their aggression, and protect the men they keep kidnapping, breaking our human trafficking laws. Now, go in Peace."

She stands and we are dismissed. I stand and follow my mom out the door and down a flight of stairs at the end of the hall. We go down one flight, then one more into the basement of the courthouse.

Time has stretched into a changeable, amorphous thing. Each step takes an eternity, like the seconds have thickened, but in a flash we're standing before a metal, reinforced door. My mother unlocks it and steps through ahead of me.

The room is small and bare, with a couple of lockers, a mirror, and a bench in the corner with a curtain to pull around it. My mom gives a quick squeeze to my hand again and turns to the locker, pulling out a plastic bag that she rips open. It's a set of neatly folded clothes. They look nothing like the school uniform I'm wearing.

She turns back to me. "Amity."

I wait. She takes a deep breath.

"Your name is Ami. If anyone asks, you refused the Oath and are trying to find your friend at the Forge. Stay on the depo train all the way through New York and transfer in Kingston. Get a ticket to Vancouver and from there you can catch a flight to Anchorage. Buy tickets in cash. Once you get a phone, use a secure service to text or call the number written on the note, which is sewn inside the pants with the cash." She holds open the gray pants and shows me the inside. "Open this up once you are out of Greater Maryland."

"Mom." My panic rises, bleeding through my mask. "Do I have to?"

My mom doesn't hesitate. "Yes. These are direct orders, Amity. Think of it as an opportunity to serve your country and cement your HighClear status. We knew they would be taking men today, on Oath Day. I'm sorry you're not more prepared." For the first time a hint of worry flickers over her face. "The Peaceful Society trusts you. You proved yourself at school, and now with your Oath and your dedication."

"Okay. Okay." I gather the clothes, the jeans, wool

socks, and boots. A black T-shirt with a picture I don't recognize and a black leather jacket with pockets inside and out.

"Get a phone. Keep track of your money. Keep it inside your clothes at all times. I can't give you a Taser because all weapons are removed from deportees."

"It's okay," I reassure her. I wouldn't have any idea what to do with a Taser anyway. I bring the bundle to the corner and pull the curtain, changing out of my uniform into the strange clothes. I hear my mother's breath, a little too deep, a little too even. She's trying to control herself, calm herself down.

I step out and we hug, her arms tight around my back. Despite an effort not to cry, my chest heaves as tiny gasps escape me. She buries her face in my hair, holding me almost too tight.

"My smart girl, Amity. You have to be aggressive out there, okay? Defend yourself if you need to."

I've never heard her talk like this.

"It's...different. You won't get in trouble for...yelling. For fighting back. You need to protect yourself," she whispers fiercely, as she uses a tool to unlock my SafeGuard and puts an e-watch on my wrist instead.

"Remember what you're there to do," she says finally. With one more deep breath, she turns to the door. Apologetically she takes a zip tie from her pocket. "We need to do this. Just until we get to the cell."

Oh, wow, I'm going to be restrained?

I hold my wrists out and she wraps it around, tying them together.

"We're going down one more level. You'll have to pretend you don't know me."

I nod, mute. This is happening. Her eyes sweep me one more time and she pulls a knife from her pocket. My mother carries a knife?

"Amity," she says gently. "Your braid, I'm so sorry." She swallows. "I have to cut it."

She waits, unsure, until I nod. Then she loosens my braid, rapidly slicing off my hair at my shoulders. She pulls what's left of my brown hair back, wrapping the hairband around in a ponytail. I watch her do this in the mirror.

I don't look anything like myself now. The leather jacket, my hair in a ponytail like a rebel in a government video.

"Go in Peace, Amity," my mom whispers. Shaking slightly, she leans over to lay the braid on the bench. Then she straightens, sighs, and pushes open the metal door, leading me into the hallway.

7

AMITY

I FOLLOW my mother through the basement of the courthouse, my arms cuffed in the front. I never dreamed that this day would be like this. I figured I'd pledge my Oath, grab my bags, and head to the Institute to start training.

Instead, I'm dressed like an Oath Refuser. My wrists are bound like a criminal. I have a rebel haircut. I'm about to be deported.

My mom's back straightens as another Officer passes us, barely looking up. I see my mom sigh with relief, a slight slump, and then she steels herself as the noise grows at the end of the hall.

There's a murmur of voices, and the sound sends a shiver up my spine. I'm used to the low, soothing voices of my teachers at City College High School, and the mostly— well—partially controlled voices of my friends trying to follow the rules and speak without aggression.

This sounds nothing like that. The murmur swells,

spiking with outbursts of yelling, people talking, loud and angry. There's the high-pitched sound of a woman crying and she sounds scared, hysterical. There's a rumble of a man talking that grows to an angry, bellowing conclusion.

My mother has slowed down, and I've slowed behind her. We turn a corner and there's a wide-open area behind bars with hundreds of people. They're sitting on benches or on the floor. Some of them are standing or slumped against the walls.

The bars go from the floor to the ceiling, cordoning off the area. It's a holding cell. My mother's back straightens all the way, her face cold. She pulls the gate open with a jerk and stands motionless, waiting. I pause in front of her and she takes her knife out, cutting the ties off my wrists, jerking her head for me to go inside.

With wide eyes I enter the cell. No one tries to push their way out, no one interacts with my mom at all. How much time does she spend down here? Is this a regular part of her job?

I don't know what to think about this whole other side of her I'm seeing. I slip through the cell, trying to remember what she told me. I'm Ami now. Sewn into my clothes are the money and phone number I'm supposed to access once we cross the border, somewhere near Scranton. Then my mission: go to Anchorage, find Zeph, check out a group called the Forge.

I don't know how to do any of this. It's quite impossible. I don't think they could have picked a worse person for this mission. Accessing the money—the very first job—I don't have any idea how to do that. It's sewn into my pants somehow? What do I do, rip my clothes?

Adrenaline floods my system and I react automatically from my training—slow down my breathing, release the tension in my muscles. I turn to say goodbye, but all I see is my mother's retreating back. So that's how it's going to be.

My throat feels thick and swollen. I move through the room aimlessly. It's a large space, filled with murmurs and shouts.

There are all different kinds of people. I'm used to the long braids of my teachers and the CSOs, all women in Positions of Power. The WPA men like my dad have short hair and easy smiles.

The people here all look different. Everyone's in street clothes like me, not a uniform in sight. A lot of them are pretty haggard. Tired looking, worn, not like the Citizens I see around my neighborhood.

My self-control spins away from me. Each time I tug my breathing and heart rate to slow down, my adrenaline spikes all over again and the panic rises. Yes, the people are different, but it's also super crowded. The sound of voices rising and falling, the unexpected outbursts of anger and glee, and the arguments keep me on edge.

In the back I find an open spot at the edge of a bench. I'll sit here and wait.

"Okay, kiddo, almost time," says a voice next to me.

I turn. I'm not sure who's the kid here. The person looks no older than me, and maybe younger. Their body is lean and lanky, and I can't tell if it's a boy or a girl. Even their hair seems confused; it's cut short to the scalp on one side and hangs in a shaggy wave on the other. They are wearing purple overalls over a baggy shirt and a hoodie with orange flowers scattered across it.

"Get there yet?" they ask, sounding annoyed.

"What do you mean?" I respond. *What is happening here?*

"Did you figure me out? Which box to put me in?"

I freeze. I don't want to offend anyone. Did I break an unspoken rule by staring? Their outfit is...striking.

"I'm, uh, I'm sorry," I stammer.

"Just kidding. Jeez, relax." They pat my knee once, sympathetically.

"I'm not a boy *or* a girl," they say, with a friendly shoulder bump. "I don't subscribe to any of that."

"Okay..." I trail off.

"Ren. Nice to meet you," they say with a grin.

"I'm Ami," I tell them. "I'm being deported."

"Oh, are you?" Ren winks, then falters. "I honestly can't tell if you're joking."

The ground feels like it's shifting under me.

"I'm not," I reassure them earnestly. "I need to get to Anchorage," I say, lowering my voice.

Ren's eyes grow big and dart around. "I hear you, kiddo, but let's be careful who we say that to, okay? Jeez, you all by yourself or what?"

For some reason my throat closes at that. I push tears back.

"Aw, Ami, I'm alone too." Ren is serious now and stares into space a second before looking back at me, shaking their head. "Stick with me, kiddo. I'm also headed," they hesitate, "north."

I nod, taking note, and Ren laughs. "You're so serious. Jeez." They glance around, craning their neck to see over everyone. People are starting to stand up, so we stand up too, but I stay near Ren.

"What's your story, got folks in Alaska?" they ask.

I remember what my mom said. "My friend—uh—refused the Oath and left. He said that's where he's going. I want to find him if I can."

Ren nods as we line up. There's a big loading dock outside a garage door that's open at the back of the room. Buses are pulling up to the dock and people are filing on.

"I hope you find your friend," they say. Then we're quiet. I'm about to find out what it's like to be deported.

Bored-looking Officers stand at the entrance to the buses. There are metal detectors set up. A man in front of me walks through one and it beeps. The Officer holds out a small bin with a frown, and the man sighs and takes his earrings out, dropping them in.

He walks through again in silence and on the other side he turns back to the Officer but she sternly jerks her head towards the bus, shoving a bag into his hand. There's an unspoken staring match until the man turns, boarding the bus with a muttered curse.

I think about the money sewn inside my pants and realize I'm sweating. There's no metal in there, right? My mom wouldn't put me in that situation. Of course, I never would have thought I'd get deported either, so I'm not a great judge of what plans my mom has in place for me.

I glance at Ren who nods with a frown.

"If you're hiding anything it's not too late to drop it."

I shake my head and Ren reaches up to the ear hidden under their curtain of hair and pulls out a small hoop.

"Here you go. Enjoy!" they say to the CSO, almost a

taunt, but with a winning smile. Rather than take offense, the Officer laughs and waves us through, handing the hoop back to Ren.

Despite sweating and my heart racing out of control, I walk through and there's no beep, no red light flashing at the top. The Officer gives us each a bag, which has a sad-looking sandwich and an apple.

It's crowded on the bus. There are a couple of families with kids. I wonder what they're doing here. It's the same mix of folks from back in the holding cell. Feeling out of my depth, I follow Ren, who scoots into a seat halfway back. They look up at me expectantly, so I slide in beside them. I may not know anything about Ren, but they've been friendly, so I'll stick with them, at least for now, since they're heading the same way I am.

The bus ride is super short. As we pull up to Penn Station we're herded off the bus by Security Officers and down to a platform. It's the same deal, metal detectors. This time it goes faster and I'm on the depo train before I know it, following Ren to a pair of seats once again.

Ren slides down, bracing their knees against the back of the seat in front of us. They pull open the bag from the Officer and take a couple bites of their sandwich.

"So how'd they pick you up?" Their eyes sweep me. "Were you fighting?" they ask, their eyes lingering on the logo of my T-shirt. I wonder what the logo means.

"No," I laugh reflexively. It reminds me of being in school. The teacher would hear raised voices and come over with that same question, "Were you fighting?" It was never me. But if someone got caught they could be in mandatory therapy for the rest of the week.

"Definitely not," I add. "But I Refused my Oath."

Ren stares at me, then lowers their voice. "Ami, we're going for tough here. Let me help you with that answer," they whisper. "I'll say, 'Were you fighting?' You say, 'Yeah.'"

They sit up straight. "Were you fighting?" they ask again, their voice raised.

Every bone in my body is telling me to deny, deny, deny.

"Yeah," I say. It comes out of my mouth with difficulty.

"What about you?" I ask, not sure what the polite response is in this situation.

Ren shrugs. "I'm a writer. I wrote something that was kinda violent."

"How did the Peaceful Society find out?" I ask.

"The PS? Well, it was really good, kiddo. A lot of people read it. I write a lot, and most of it isn't about the joys of maidenhood, chastity, and dumb men. It's about violence," they say in a stage whisper. "And fighting." They laugh as I barely suppress a shudder.

"Oh, Ami, so green. Ren will protect you." With that their grin slips and Ren looks upset. Then they straighten, smiling with their mouth but not their eyes. "Maybe you'll star in one of my stories one day."

"Maybe," I say.

"I'm taking a nap. Wake me up when we hit the border," Ren announces, bunching up their hoodie and slumping against the window.

I'm on my own. I find myself sitting rigidly and force myself to relax, sag a little, act like I belong here. I try to get into the mindset of Ami, but the best I can do is watch out the window in silence and hope no one says anything to me.

8

AMITY

PENNSYLVANIA HAS a lot of farms and mountains. At one point I see a helicopter, something I've never seen outside of videos. I lean over Ren to stick my face up to the window, watching the blades spin faster than I can see, the body painted green and gray.

I wonder if it's a Peaceful Society helicopter. It has a vaguely threatening look to it. I've heard that rich people up in New England use them to travel around, although with high-speed trains and ebuses I can't imagine wanting to be suspended in the air with all that noise and danger.

Ren clears their throat and I scoot back.

"Sorry! I've never seen a helicopter before."

"Aw. Getting out into the world for the first time, Ami."

Ren uses my new nickname and I flinch. Ren glances at me sharply.

"Not your only name?" Ren asks in a low voice, close to my ear. I shrug. Ren hesitates a minute, then gives me a wry smile.

"I have another name too. Serenity." Their lips purse nervously.

I nod, trying to stay matter of fact. Serenity is a common female name in the Peaceful Society. I'm not sure what to say, so I wait. I wish I could share my name back, but I don't. Ren's look is searching before they chuckle a little.

"Dumb name, really. I don't use it anymore," Ren adds carelessly.

"I like Ren," I tell them, and I do. It fits them. A strong, lean name, soft in the mouth.

Ren nods once and turns back to the window.

The mountains are bigger here, the hillsides are a thick, bright green. Ren cranes their head to see ahead.

"The border's coming up. You ready, kiddo?"

My stomach flips and I connect right away with my breath, slowing down, steadying myself.

Ren grins widely. "You're good at that, aren't you?"

"At what?" I ask, breathing through my nose to regulate my breath.

"All that mindful non-reactivity stuff. PS I'm-A-Robot garbage."

I giggle nervously. "I don't think that's what it's called."

"You know, PS for Passive Submission."

"Ren!" I exclaim, knocking my shoulder into theirs.

"Pliant Subordination?"

"Okay, okay, that's enough," I whisper, scandalized.

Ren waits a beat and tilts their chin proudly at me as I repress the giggles that threatened to overtake me.

"That works too, right?" they ask.

"What does?"

"You know, humor. Not everything has to be repressed, Ami. Sometimes you can just laugh about it."

Unconventional. But they're not wrong. I feel better, lighter, not as nervous about crossing the border.

The bus slows to a stop while I'm still grinning to myself. I rub my leg, feeling the inside pocket with the money. It's all I have to go on at this point, besides a weird seatmate and incomplete knowledge of how the real world works.

The road is closed ahead. A big sign says WELCOME TO NEW YORK under layers of graffiti. Next to it a newer sign marks the border of the Peaceful Society and entry into New England.

The doors in the front open and two CSOs sweep on board, weapons on their backs and their belts. They wait for the last murmurs on to die down. Then one speaks in a quiet voice.

"Please be ready. Your face will be scanned, and your watch if you have one. As a deportee of the Peaceful Society you must petition the government for reentry, including a hearing and the presentation of evidence and character witnesses. This information can be found at stations along the border of our territory."

The women start down the aisle of the bus with handheld face scanners. None of us have a SafeGuard—those were all removed before we were deported—but lots of people have e-watches like the one my mom put on me.

You can't have a phone for private use in Greater Maryland. I've heard about phones and e-glasses and tablets and everything, but we were taught in school that peace and safety was more important than what my teachers called "certain kinds of entertainment."

They stop at a boy ahead of me.

"Do you have any proof of identification?" one Officer asks him, patient. The boy shakes his head. With a small sigh the CSO sneaks a glance at the other Officer and leans down to talk to the boy in a lower voice.

"I can issue you an e-watch. You'll need it in Canada to access just about anything." She goes to unzip a pouch at her belt but the boy declines it.

"I don't—I won't need it. Don't waste it on me, save it for someone else. I'll be fine," he reassures her.

I glance at Ren in question but they shake their head slightly and I do more "PS stuff" to calm myself and refocus on the seat ahead of me.

When the Officers get to us, Ren and I stick our watches and look up into the face scanner. The Officer has no reaction whatsoever. I'm not sure if she knows my secret or not, she gives no indication.

When they get to the back of the train car they turn and walk back up the aisle, eyes sweeping over all of the people tucked into the seats. They turn back one more time and the Officer says simply, "Go in Peace."

A couple people murmur it back, me included. It's a refrain that's been drilled into us since we were kids, but Ren stays pointedly silent. We both let out a deep sigh when the door clicks shuts. With a gentle tug the train starts forward again.

We drive a short distance and stop, the first stop in New York. A bunch of people get off and new people get on. It's a lot of work boots and flannel shirts.

I've heard about New England. New York and the northern states rejected most technology after the Integration. The New England territory gives their Citizens much more freedom and privacy than the Peaceful Society, but only after they completed a huge reengineering project to decommission most of the public infrastructure around networks and the internet. Their cell phone towers were taken down and dismantled.

Everyone up here communicates over old-fashioned phone lines. Sometimes my mom talks about how my grandmother would have felt right at home in New England. None of the New Yorkers are wearing an e-watch.

When the train starts up again, I'm ready. It's time to access the money that's sewn into my pants. I tell Ren I'm heading to the bathroom and lurch my way to the back of the train car.

I slide the door open and step inside. It's brown, small, and cramped. I use the bathroom and reach down into my pants, feeling for the tell-tale weight of the packet sewn in. I contort, trying to figure out the best way to access what's inside.

The stitches at the top, closing up the top of the pocket, are loose. I tug at the thread and it breaks easily, and I keep tugging and ripping until I can wedge my hand inside and slide out an envelope.

I gently tear the envelope, easing it open. There are a ton of Peaceful Society bills in here—100s, more money than I've ever seen. There's a different currency also, maybe Canadian money.

The other thing is a note with a ten-digit number written on it. I put it all into a different pocket inside my jacket that zips up. Great. The next step is to see about getting a cell phone. I don't think I can buy one in New York, or use it in New England, but I'll need to contact this number once I get into Canada and I'm on the network there.

I head back to my seat. The sun is dipping lower in the sky, but the days are long this time of year.

Ren is swiping on their watch and looks up. "There you are, Ami."

"I'm back," I agree. "Hey, Ren," I whisper. "I need to buy a cell phone."

Ren nods. "Yeah, if you're going north, definitely."

"Uh...how do I do that?" I ask.

Ren's eyes shift around.

"Well, kiddo, you can get one in Canada. Or there's probably someone on the train selling them, rebels in the dining car. I bought one on the train last time, black market."

"You've been deported before?"

Ren frowns. "Yeah." They sigh, shaking their head. "And yet I came back."

"Why?" I ask quietly.

"My brother," they say after a pause. The pain in their eyes and the fact that they're here alone tells me a lot.

They change the subject. "Do you want to see about a phone?"

"Um, yeah. Which way is the dining car?" I say, feeling a little sick all the sudden.

Ren snorts. They must see my face fall because they reassure me.

"Hey, kiddo. Ren's not going to send you off to the dining car by yourself. We'll go together. Cell phone's going to cost you, though."

"I got it," I reassure them. "But Ren, you don't have to—"

"I'll come," they assure me. "I want to help. Call it paying it forward if you need to. If my brother escapes, he'll need all the help he can get."

"Well, okay," I say slowly.

"Great. Let's go."

"Oh, right now?" I ask, surprised.

"No...right *now*." Ren gets up as they say it, and it happens again. They made me laugh, and it's hard for me to be anxious when I laugh.

Feeling a bit nervous, and excited, I follow Ren up to the front of the car and wait as they slide the door open to step between the train cars.

MARCH 16, 2017

I want to bring attention to two different groups working to reduce violence in Baltimore ("Lawsuits mount over police"). On one hand we have the Baltimore Gun Task Force. This plainclothes group of police has been accused of stealing guns, drugs, and money from criminals *and* victims of violence in Baltimore.

On the other hand the non-profit I belong to, Mothers Against Violence, has not taken a single gun away or made any arrests. However, we have brought over 5,000 meals to victims, held nearly 700 mediation meetings, made over 1,000 hospital visits, and raised 4 million dollars, every dollar spent to repair harm done by gun violence.

Shootings are down 25% from this time last year and thousands of MAV members have made the pledge of nonviolence. The new law signed last week by the president will require trigger locks and background checks in every state. No gun will be sold in our country without a background check. No gun will be carried without a trigger lock.

Join Mothers Against Violence as we change the future of Baltimore. We will become a city without violence, a city without guns. Find out more at MAVBaltimore.com.

Sincerely,
Mikayla Adamson
Mothers Against Violence

9

VALE

I GET BACK onto the highway. There are cops out, and I see someone pulled over. We're on the lookout for the PS, but I don't think they have jurisdiction here in Ohio. Whenever I see flashing lights I tense a little, and I can't stop watching for them even when we switch drivers and I'm in the passenger seat.

"Looks like we got away pretty clean that time," Mark says, a little uncertain.

I'm not known for making conversation—I find it pretty difficult. I prefer someone give me orders or explain how to do something, rather than expect me to answer them.

"Not that guy." I state the obvious. Sure, we might have gotten away, but it wasn't a clean mission. We lost a man, and he may have compromised future rescues.

"What do you think they'll do to him?" he asks.

I shake my head. My guess is as good as his. How can I end this conversation and not have to talk anymore? "He'll be sent to a camp."

"Oh." Mark finally stops trying to engage me in conversation. I hear a murmur in the back, but I'm not tempted to listen and try to join in.

I pull a map out of the glove compartment and take a look. I think we'll stop in Toledo. I can get a few hours of sleep before we start the trek across Canada, and the others can clean out the van, pick up some food to bring along.

Most of these guys have probably never been out of the PS and don't realize how things are in the Midwest. It's a pretty sweet setup. I won't lie and say I haven't thought about moving down here someday. The climate is milder than Anchorage, for sure. But despite the good vibes, equality of the sexes, and a lot of freedom to pursue individual interests thanks to their universal basic income, it's still lacking something.

When an animal has nothing to fear—no predator, no lack of food, no conflict in their surroundings—they start to lie around. Look at animals in zoos and how they start to hurt themselves or act in unnatural ways. Zookeepers have to give them drugs to calm them down and help with their anxiety.

My dad and I discuss this a lot. He thinks humans get it wrong when they think safety will make people feel good. It's the whole problem with the PS. For one thing, they don't know when to stop. They won't be satisfied until they put a chip in everyone's brain and force them to be at peace all the time.

But there's always people who thrive in dangerous environments, taking risks, like the wild animals I see in Alaska.

As comfortable as it is here in Ohio, they lost

something just like the rest of the world when they signed the Universal Accord.

That thing they lost, that's what the Forge wants to bring back. We will forge a new world, where life isn't about waiting to die, but about people having control over their own lives. They can choose to do great things or terrible things, and face the consequences of the choices they make.

The PS thinks we want to bring the guns back, but the guns are only part of it. We want to bring back a world where something can happen. Where every day is not one after another spent online if you're in Canada, in some community center learning German or pottery in the Midwest, or tending your garden in the PS.

In an hour we pull up to a motel that's next to a community center. They kept a lot of tech here, letting AI take care of their governing and planning.

Once robots could run the service sector—making coffee, fixing plumbing, even giving a great massage—they got UBI organized and focused on hobbies and sports and the kinds of things that bring people together and give them something to do. My dad says everyone in the Midwest is retired. Like, everyone.

We check into the motel and Mark and I grab a quick nap in the room.

The guys do a decent job cleaning up the van. I try to smile but end up giving them a nod with a not-frown, which should be enough. Might as well get them used to the way things will be up north. We head over to the community center.

I catch up to the guy who was at the courthouse with Amity Bloome. I guess I'm still thinking about her. He has red hair and pale skin, and he's humming quietly to himself. He's kept the SafeGuard we took off him, the fake, and he's fiddling with it while we cross the street. I let my eyes linger on his hands and I'm surprised to see he's managed to reset the device. He's programming user information.

"What are you doing?" I ask him.

The kid, Zeph, gets a little redder, if that's possible, but doesn't stop typing and scrolling on the little watch-shaped device.

"It's an interesting design," he says. "Double encryption?"

"Did you learn about that in the PS?" I didn't think they let men in on the design of their security apparatus.

He looks up. "PS. What's that?"

"The Peaceful Society," I clarify.

"Oh." His fingers finish and he slips the SafeGuard into his pocket. "I taught myself. Took things apart, found some old programming books. I like figuring out how things work," he admits.

"Then it's good you're getting out of there," I say, surprising myself with all this chatting.

"I guess." He looks conflicted. "There are people I'll miss."

I wonder if he means Amity. And just like that I'm thinking about her again, tall and tan and freckled, and the minty smell that clung to her.

"Maybe I'll go back someday," he says a little wistfully.

"Maybe." I'm doubtful.

We reach the door to the community center and head inside. It's crowded this time of evening, with people on exercise bikes in a windowed room to our right. A long table in another room shows a spirited discussion and a whiteboard, and there are steps down to a library that's bustling with parents and children. They do have some nice resources out here.

We head to the kitchen where we're picking up a food order that should get us across the border and most of the way through Canada. The big box is heavy with packaged meals and wrapped-up sandwiches. I don't have to pay because that's all been arranged ahead of time by the Forge.

A couple of people are working in the kitchen and a girl closes the fridge. She's pretty, with long braids and a nice figure. My eyes rest on her while I'm thinking about the drive across Canada, but I guess she takes that as an invitation and gives me a flirty look, running her eyes up and down me.

I sigh and turn away. I'm on the clock, and frankly, there's something about me that can't get interested in someone I just met. My dad says when the Adamson men fall, they fall hard and forever.

I know he'll be carrying a torch for my mom forever, even if he has women stay with him sometimes at the Forge. I don't even go that far. It's hard to trust people, and I don't want a girl in my private room. The thought makes me nauseous, actually, although I'd never admit it.

I try not to show any disgust on my face, this girl

doesn't deserve that. I turn away and quickly herd the men back outside.

"Eat something, then we head to the border," I grunt and grab a sandwich to eat at a picnic table. It's still light out, but it's getting later and I'm surprised how many people are out and about in town. When I see a mom and dad holding the hands of a little boy my chest feels tight, but I push it down.

It's a sweet little Black boy with his parents enjoying the walk home from his piano lesson or whatever they were doing. His parents look down on him with so much pride, it's like the three of them are in a bubble of happiness together. It feels so familiar.

I had that. That little boy was me ten years ago. Full of love, full of optimism. Heading into a future that would be better, safer, and more peaceful.

I know my mother worked so hard to leave me that legacy. Little did she know how wrong things would go, how her own organization and government would turn on her once she started to expose their hypocrisy. How dark my father would become without her.

I shiver and hope that boy stays in his bubble, and nothing ever comes to burst it.

10

AMITY

REN STEPS SMOOTHLY between the train cars. There's a platform with rails to hold on to. The wind whips up the minute I'm in the doorway. It's scary, but I watch what they do carefully and step, clutching the rail tightly and managing the second step into the next car, pulling the door closed behind me.

Ren grins. "Good work."

It's a whole new, crowded train car full of unfamiliar faces. From the look of things, it's a mix of deportees from the Peaceful Society and a bunch of New England folks.

There are more men than women in New England. They come from Philadelphia, Baltimore, and Washington, DC, the cities that make up the Peaceful Society. Somehow even with all those men they manage to keep the peace, but we hear stories. It's different up here.

Ren stands tall as they move through the crowd. Their hoodie has pockets and a zipper and they tug the zipper all the way to their neck and run a hand through their hair.

I'm reminded of Zeph and recognize the fidgeting as nerves. I appreciate that Ren is willing to come and help me.

I prepare myself mentally that getting a phone might not work out right now. The people we talk to could be rude, or mean, or scary. I can try again in Canada, I plan as a backup.

We do the same thing again, moving to the next car. It feels easier this time and Ren slides into a seat in the back, speaking in a low voice to a woman I've never seen before. She glances up at me and I freeze, standing in the aisle. I'm not sure what's happening right now. There's more whispered conference and then Ren straightens back up, leading the way. Standing before the door into the next train car, they turn.

"The dining car has a group of guys from Anchorage that sell stuff off the books. For the right price they'll probably have a wiped phone you can use."

I nod. Ren runs their hand through their hair again, nervous.

"Just, uh, try to answer their questions as honestly as... makes sense. But don't say more than you need," they suggest.

I reach into my coat. "I could give you the money and you could..."

Ren's face twists. "Sorry, kiddo, I'll go in with you, but I'm not interested in buying anything from these guys today." They say it with finality. "If this is what you want, you'd better handle it." Their eyebrows draw together and I can tell Ren's worried.

"You don't *have* to do this, Ami," they whisper.

But these are my instructions. This is my next task. I can do it. I start my breathing, fast in, slow out, and Ren gives me a wink.

"PS for Patiently Spineless..."

I can't hold back a chuckle, and as the tension breaks a little, Ren pushes the door open and steps through.

The next train car is all men. My eyes sweep the room slowly, trying to make it look casual. I don't see a single woman here.

The men are sitting together all around, eating and drinking and talking loudly. There's a group playing cards in a booth.

In the back, a cluster of men have papers and a map scattered across their table. It's loud. There's a counter with a stooped man behind it, standing in front of bottles and packages lined up on shelving.

Ren lets their body slouch a little, looking more relaxed, and I immediately copy them. A few heads turn but we're mostly ignored. The eyes lingering on me make me shudder. Ren leads me through the car to the counter where the stooped man dries his hands on a towel, turning to us.

"Get you all something?" he says without expression.

Ren tilts their head to me, indicating I should answer. I make eye contact carefully.

"I'd like to buy a cell phone," I tell him. He doesn't react. Then his eyes flick to something behind me, and he shrugs.

"I hear they have them in Canada." He checks his watch. "We'll be there soon."

He turns away but I stay rooted. Ren told me about the

difference between the kinds of cell phones. Whatever I buy in Canada will be overseen by the CGC, the Canadian Government Corporation, and what I need is a wiped phone that can use the infrastructure but not be tracked.

"I'm looking for a wiped phone," I say to his back.

The man still doesn't reply. You'd think we were back in the Peaceful Society with all this deliberate non-reactivity. He turns to the table behind me, the one with the papers and maps.

Someone approaches and the man behind the counter turns away again. This time, with something like a flinch. I turn and start.

It's an older version of the guard I saw with Zeph, the boy whose name is on the tip of my tongue. He has the same deep brown skin, deep-set eyes with long lashes, and strong brow. The lines on his face are deeper, and there are streaks of gray in his closely cropped hair. His mouth has a pinched, cruel tilt to it. He notices my obvious reaction.

"Have we met before?" he asks in a low, raspy voice.

"No," I answer. Then I remember Ren telling me to be honest. "You look like someone I met in Baltimore."

The man grins and it doesn't improve things at all. Even Ren flinches beside me, as they try to appear interested in the card game going on by the window.

"You've met Vale," he says and his eyes narrow.

Vale! That was his name, Vale Adamson. I remember his mom's warm voice now, calling him to come to the car after meetings. What happened to them, and why is the son of a MAV leader working for rebels?

I shrug, breathing through my nose, and hope I'm keeping a straight face. "Vale, yeah."

He stares at me, silent, and a crawling sensation creeps up my arms. His head swivels to the man behind the counter.

"She says she wants to buy a wiped phone," the stooped man tells him.

"What's your name?" the man who looks like Vale asks me in his low voice.

"Ami," I answer softly. I remember I'm supposed to be a rebel sympathizer, an Oath Refuser, and I straighten my shoulders.

"And where are you going, Ami?" he asks, not giving me his name.

"Anchorage," I tell him and close my mouth to stop myself from saying more.

He nods. "Then we'll be seeing more of each other."

I'm not sure what that means. I try not to flinch from his sharp gaze. I have a million tells. My ears, unpierced. My hair, all-natural color. No tattoos to speak of. I don't look like the other deportees.

At least my clothes are worn and blend in, but I can tell that the years of Citizen training, my posture, my expressions, my breathing must show through. This man doesn't miss anything.

He decides. "Get her one, on the house," he directs the man behind the counter. Unreactive as ever, the stooped man moves to open a low drawer behind him, his body blocking me from seeing what's in it.

"I'm happy to pay," I say, imbuing my voice with strength.

"Let's call it a favor," he rasps. I don't want to owe this man a favor, but I don't want to say no to him.

Next to me Ren gives a sharp nod. "Thanks," they say and I echo them, "Thank you."

"How was he?" the man asks, leaning closer.

I freeze to prevent myself from jerking back, then ask curiously, "Who?"

"Vale, in the PS. You said you saw him in Baltimore. Was he working as a guard? Or in the WPA?"

"As a guard," I confirm. "Is he your...?" I trail off, not sure what to ask. They certainly look related.

"Son," he confirms. "Vale is my son. I haven't seen him in weeks. How did he look?" An anxious twist comes over his face. I smile back before I can second-guess myself, thinking about Vale.

"He looked good. He looked...well." He was gorgeous is what he was. Just as handsome as the older man next to me, but without the scary vibe.

I remember how his eyes followed me, the quiet way he stood with his fingers on the skin of my wrist. I still don't understand how he got involved with whatever this is— Ren called them a militia group.

I've been staring off into space and I suddenly worry that Vale's father can read my thoughts somehow, but his eyes are also blank. Does he miss his son? Why was Vale "gone" for weeks? If this man says he'll see me in Anchorage, does that mean Vale will be there—and Zeph too?

"He was traveling with someone I'm looking for, someone named Zeph, with red hair." I search the man's face for answers but he just shakes his head, frowning.

"No idea."

Maybe I can get the answers I need from Vale and his

group when I get to Alaska, the information the Peaceful Society wants. Then I can go back and have a normal life with Ethan and my mom and dad, or join the other HighClear girls at the Institute, and not be on this crazy mission.

I correct myself; it's not a crazy mission. The reason the Peaceful Society sent me is because I was close to Zeph. If anyone can earn his trust and find out more about the group that brainwashed him and stole him away, it's me. We can keep more men safe, keep more families together.

I glance around at the men in the room. A few meet my eyes; they were staring at me. I suddenly want to leave this train car, find a spot back with the deportees and farmers, and leave all these men behind, with their loud voices and roving eyes.

The stooped man behind the counter hands me a box. He opens the lid and I see a smooth silver case. He takes a pen out and scribbles something on the box.

"Code," he mutters to me and Ren nods. I guess they know what that means.

Vale's father heads back to the booth. "I'm sure I will see you again, Ami." He nods to Ren but doesn't say anything to them.

"I'm Isaiah Adamson," he continues. "My organization is called the Forge, and we're available if you need anything once you get to Anchorage."

Ren stiffens but I coach myself through staying loose, keeping my eyes on his as I nod. Maybe he thought this would scare me, but I simply thank him for the phone one more time and move back through the car.

I feel his eyes on my back. Maybe not just his, and I

can't get through the opening into the next car fast enough. Ren pulls me through the aisle and the next car until we find an empty seat and slide in. This time I'm next to the window. I hand the box to Ren and bend forward over my knees, breathing deeply, my face in my hands.

"Jeez, Ami, that was crazy," Ren mutters.

I'm shaking.

"You're okay, you're okay." Ren rubs my back. They pull off their hoodie and bunch it up, pushing it into my arms where I squeeze it tight.

"You did it, Ami, you got your phone. Now let's take it easy for the rest of New York, okay?"

11

AMITY

CROSSING the border into Canada is much faster than leaving the Peaceful Society. Someone from New England gets on board and asks if we have any questions and that's it. Privacy is such a thing here they apparently don't scan you or keep track of your movements.

I'm not sure how they keep everyone safe. Someone could be hurting someone else right now in some unsupervised home in Massachusetts. It used to happen all the time before the Integration.

I've heard murmurs back home about this, concern for the weaker citizens in the other territories: the children, the teenagers, the elderly. But all the territories comply with the Universal Accord: they abolished guns, so I guess that's enough.

I wonder—if men grew up with the old ways, wielding power over other people, reacting with violence when they feel scared or threatened—how will they unlearn those behaviors without Citizen training?

How will they pass on peace to the next generation without government oversight of schools and learning? My mom says they're just sweeping violence under the rug in New England, and not establishing a new legacy like the Peaceful Society.

At least, considering the lax security at the border, it seems like folks can leave if they don't like it.

Canada is...different. Canada was consolidated by the Canadian Government Corporation after signing the Universal Accord. They dismantled their military, sure, but they didn't start regulating tech the way the territories in the old United States did.

You see the difference immediately when we cross the St. Lawrence River. There are big signs outside next to the train, wide and tall, with high-res screens flashing pictures of people laughing and running, and advertisements for clothes, makeup, and vacations.

They're like the videos the Peaceful Society makes but instead of citizen education, they're directing people to buy things: a headset, a pair of shoes, a tiny apartment with a virtual reality pod, and a food delivery service all flash on the screen in quick succession.

I turn to Ren. "This is overwhelming." Ren doesn't even blink.

"Do you want to switch seats?" they ask. "It's all garbage, Ami, don't even give it the time of day. Don't let them draw you into that nonsense. Vipers."

"How does anyone have the money to buy that stuff? Where do they put it?" I ask as Ren scootches by me to take the place by the window and we awkwardly change places.

They shake their head. "Most of the stuff never sells. I think people find it comforting to see the ads, have that feeling of desire, the hope that something out there will make you feel better."

I shake my head in confusion.

"Look, I'm no expert, but most of the money in Canada just gets passed around their virtual marketplace. People pay each other, pay for upgrades, new experiences, trying to feel good. Have you done VR?"

My answer must show on my face.

Ren laughs. "Virtual reality. You can go into one of those pods and live your life in there. They'll bring you food, they'll bring you to a bathroom. You can stay there all the time. It's cold up here. Some folks think VR's more fun than reality."

I try to imagine sitting in a pod all day.

"It's so different from New England," I muse, trying to fit all the new information into my understanding.

"Yeah, New England's got nothing. They ripped all the fiber out."

I'm so confused, even as the train slows to a stop.

"Hang on, when we get to Kingston I'll show you," Ren says.

A minute later we stand up and I hand Ren their hoodie that I've been clutching since the whole phone-buying adventure.

Ren scoots past me and leads the way up the aisle to the door. We climb down and stare around the station. There are screens everywhere. I'm trying to see where to go, when the train starts to pull away behind us.

"Ren!" I clutch their arm in alarm, but they reassure me.

"Don't worry, kiddo, we have to switch to the trans-Canada anyway. Let's look around first, then we'll catch it later. And it won't have those guys from the Forge," they add in a low voice.

That sounds like a great idea. I gaze up and down, trying to take it all in.

"Welcome to Canada, kiddo," Ren says grandly. "Let me show you around."

"Have you been here before?" I ask.

"Sure, came through on my way to Anchorage last time. That's where I'm based. It's nice to be deported, actually," they tell me. "The depo train brings you all the way here."

"I guess that's nice."

Ren pulls me around a corner inside the station and into an elevator. There are videos of people in their underwear playing on the wall, advertisements for VR games and role plays.

I close my eyes, not used to the onslaught of flashing images, the people so beautiful and larger than life, the dramatic close-ups of faces and bodies and the vibrant, saturated color.

When we step out of the elevator and head outside it's muted tones of green and brown.

This doesn't look anything like the carefully cultivated gardens back home, or the wild forests of New England. It's scrubby, overgrown. It's clean but...sad. We head down the road, the sidewalk cracked with weeds shoving their way through.

In town there are clusters of screens. I don't see many

people. There's one other guy with a hat pulled low over his eyes, looking like he hopped on in New York. He disappears down an alley between two buildings and it's only Ren and me.

"Where are all the people?" I ask Ren. I'd peek in the windows to find them, but there are none of those either. It makes me nervous. "And where are the windows?"

"The new architecture." Ren shrugs. "Very efficient."

I blink. "It's so ugly."

"Take out your phone," Ren urges. "I need coffee and snacks, there must be a place." I hand Ren my phone, not quite knowing what to do with it.

Ren swipes on the screen, then stops walking, turning back to where we saw the man disappear down the alley. "It's down there."

"What's down there?" I wonder.

"The coffee shop." Ren watches my face carefully and laughs at what they see there. Ren's laugh is throaty and warm. It relaxes me immediately.

"Ever had coffee, little PS princess?" they ask.

I straighten. I'm not a Peaceful Society princess. I'm a rebel. I'm dressed like one, at least.

"Sure," I say. I've never had coffee. All drugs are strictly forbidden back home. Even chocolate, which my mom talks about sometimes, was banned for having low amounts of caffeine, and coffee is definitely not allowed.

The Society decided that any drug that would cause a change to the way you feel or act would be banned.

We get to a door with an open sign and Ren jerks it open. Inside it's pretty and warm. The walls shimmer a little—they're screens but the picture they show is beautiful, warm wooden beams and stonework and a fake window to a garden beyond, like an old-fashioned nook somewhere.

The smell in here is earthy and smoky and I take a long breath in. A man sits in a chair behind a counter, wearing a pair of e-glasses and waving his hands in the air with motions I don't recognize. There's no sign of the man we saw on the street.

On the other side of the room are several sliding doors, some closed, some open. Inside are more screens. I poke my head in curiously and Ren chuckles.

"You can drink your coffee anywhere in the world, there's even VR goggles and gloves."

I guess people close the doors and drink their coffee in tiny rooms. The rooms are so small, I do not want to sit in there. Ren asks the man in the chair for two coffees and he pulls off his glasses with a sigh and a pointed look at a touchscreen we didn't use.

"Sorry, could we get one with cream and sugar?" Ren asks, no apology in their voice. The man, sighing again, pulls two mugs from under the counter, muttering about foreigners, and fills them with a dark, shiny liquid.

"Sweet one's for her," Ren says, tilting their head to indicate me.

I shrug. I wouldn't know, but I trust Ren. We pick up our mugs. Mine is warm in my hand. It feels good after the chill in the air outside. Once we pay, the man sits down in the chair in a bit of a huff and puts his glasses back on, his arm coming up to swipe in the air, maybe playing a game.

Ren stares a minute before pushing on the door. "Come on, let's go sit on the bench."

Outside the door there are a couple of benches and a lonely tree, green and squished between the gray, windowless buildings. A chorus of chirps comes from it, a flock of tiny sparrows poking around in its leaves.

We sit down and I take a sip of the coffee. It's warm and creamy with a rich, bitter undertone and I love it. I drink a few more sips and right away there's a difference, a tingling. Caffeine is a stimulant, and this drink has a lot of it, or I'm not used to it.

Ren groans in apparent pleasure. "Oh, sweet coffee, I missed you," they whisper to their mug. I settle back on the bench, watching the birds and listening to the quiet. You would never believe we were in the middle of a town.

"It's so quiet," I remark to Ren.

"They've got the good tech, kiddo. I've only been a few places in Canada but this is pretty much what it's like now. The cities are more active...maybe." There's doubt on their face.

I shiver. I'd rather live in New England than here. This is weird. We see one person walk by wearing the same e-glasses as the person in the shop. They gesture in the air with both hands and I shake my head.

"At least there's coffee," I muse.

Ren sighs and points to my phone.

"Let's get you started on this thing, okay? Here, I'll show you how it works."

MARCH 6, 2018

Johns Hopkins University wants to make a private police force for their campus. ("Johns Hopkins University pushing bill to create its own police force in Baltimore"). I do not work for the university, nor do I live in the neighborhood, but I listen to the voices of those who will be affected and I hear a great deal of concern.

The university believes their private police will keep their community safer. Those of us in the general public wonder who is being protected from whom. The residents of Baltimore ask Hopkins to put its efforts toward making the *entire* community safer. They can do this by supporting the peace movement led by Mothers Against Violence.

Because the public has so little control over private police, Mothers Against Violence is supporting the Update to Gun Licensing bill in the Maryland legislature this spring.

Whether it's public police, private police, or private security, every person who carries a gun should have to complete strict training. Our state requires nearly 100 hours of classes and practice to get a driver's license, but the gun safety course is only 16 hours. Guns are just as dangerous as cars, and our bill will bring new standards for getting and keeping a license to buy or carry a gun in Maryland.

Join members of MAV this weekend in Annapolis to make it harder, not easier, to carry guns in our community. If Hopkins moves forward to create a private police force, their officers would be subject to the new standards of training and conduct. Gather and show your support for HB368 on Saturday at noon in front of the Maryland Statehouse. Get the details at MarylandMAV.com.

Sincerely,
Mikayla Adamson
Mothers Against Violence

12

VALE

I'M DONE with this trip. The guys in the back smell terrible. The thought of that girl, Amity, back in the PS is the worst kind of itch. Allowing myself to think about her makes me want to think about her more. It shouldn't work that way.

But my mind keeps scanning for danger and snagging on her face, worried and brightly intelligent, her eyes following our abrupt departure from the PS courthouse. I start thinking about completely unrelated things, like her slightly minty, sweet smell, or the freckles still sprinkled on her nose and cheeks.

The kids used to call her Pepper, not as a mean thing, I think she was okay with it. It slipped out when we were talking, but it was a mistake to acknowledge that I recognized her. Her mom is a big-time Soldier in the PS now. That means Amity is nothing but trouble and I need to stop thinking about her.

I also need to get out of this van. I'm the one driving as

we roll up to the gates of the Forge compound. They're all asleep, which makes it easier.

I roll my window down to confer with the guy in the security booth, then head over to intake. These men will have to prove themselves, and frankly it won't be easy. If they don't make the cut they can try their luck with the Brotherhood or up in Fairbanks. There's a lot of work up there.

The Forge has high standards for our members. It's not only about physical strength and fighting ability. It's something else too, a dedication to retake the democratic world that was stolen from us. Do whatever is necessary.

I turn on the van's overhead light.

"Okay, everyone. Out."

They rub their eyes, even Mark. He shakes the sleep off first and starts opening up the doors.

Some of the men have backpacks or other bags with them, some have nothing. They'll be provided for while they're here.

The excitement of getting out of the PS and Canada is gone now. They look worried, unsure.

"You'll sleep it off first," I tell them, to sighs of relief. "Take a shower, for God's sake," I add, rolling my window down. It was a long drive. It took close to four days, even switching off at night.

Once they drag their tired bodies out and Mark ushers them through the door to the gym in this former high school complex, I slam the doors shut and hop back in. I drive down under the school where we added parking and storage for our larger machinery.

I'm tired but also wired and I think I'll train a little, hit pads if anyone's around, or punch the bag.

I park in the garage and hop on the elevator, sincerely wishing to see no one, just go straight to my room.

My wish comes true. I get up to the fourth floor and head down the hall. My rooms are in a series of offices, an old administration suite. I have a small room and a bathroom to call my own, which is more than most men have here.

It's because of my father, sure, but I've also earned it. I'm only eighteen, but I take the most dangerous missions. I come early and stay late. I try to live up to his expectations of me. Even when I fall short it's still after pushing myself to the limit, sometimes physically, sometimes mentally.

Like the training I had to undergo to pass undercover as a guard in the PS, or blend in with loggers in New Hampshire.

If my father has a job he needs done, I can figure out how to do it for him.

My room is dark, but warm. I strip down in the bathroom and rinse the smell of the van off me, even if I'm on my way to go get sweaty again.

Water warms my back and I tip my head, letting it run over my face, down my neck and chest. Hot, scalding water. The restlessness returns and I decide to stick to my plan of heading down to train.

I dry off and hang my towel carefully, straightening it on the bar. I brush my teeth thoroughly and comb my hair.

I move to the drawers that hold my clothes. The gym clothes are the third drawer down, rows of baggy shorts folded tightly next to rolled-up sweats. On the other side, a neat array of folded T-shirts.

I take one T-shirt and one pair of shorts carefully, doing my best not to disturb the rest. I pull the clothes on and open a cupboard to find the few pairs of shoes I own besides my boots.

I grab my boxing shoes and lace them up slowly, trying to sink into the mindset. I remember I left the PS guard uniform back in the van and scribble a note to myself, putting it on my list of things to take care of tomorrow.

For tonight, I bring my gloves and hand wraps, phone and earpods, slipping my mouthguard into my pocket, and head downstairs.

The workout room is an old fitness center. There are ancient bikes and bars and plates in the back. A ring off to one side that doesn't get used much except for official fights. And there are the bags.

The floor squishes beneath my feet—mats cover most of the room. I was hoping there'd be someone down here to hit pads with, but it's empty this late so I set myself up next to the bag, slipping earpods into my ears, jumping rope to warm up.

Then, with a beat to guide me, it's not hard to get through round after round of jabs and crosses.

I move on to combinations, mixing in my hooks and body shots. I prowl around the bag, moving right and left, closing the space to practice up close, defensive. Backing up to strike from the outside, careful. Sweat starts to drip down my back and my shirt grows damp.

I grab a towel from the pile and wipe my face and arms, thoroughly warmed up. Now I focus on using more power, letting loose, listening for a loud crack exploding on the bag.

I repeat until it sounds right in my ears, until it feels right on my knuckles, sore and starting to get battered. Eventually it's time to stop. I have a million things to deal with tomorrow and it would make sense to get a few hours of sleep before then.

I can't stop. The heavy beat of the music pushes me. I punch and punch and still can't shake off the restless feeling, the pain sharper now that the skin's cracked on my knuckles, even through the gloves and hand wraps.

"Vale. Vale!" A man is behind me, shouting. I pull my earpods out, and I don't mask the fury on my face. The man draws back. He's one of my father's lieutenants.

"Your father wants to see you," he says in a quieter voice. Maybe he was saying my name a few times before I responded. I melt away the strong emotions that have me in their clutch, using a PS technique.

"Fine," I tell him. "Let me change first."

"No. He wants a report right now," he insists.

I glance down at my sweat-stained shirt and shorts. "Really? Can you give me a second?"

He shakes his head no, refusing to argue.

"Fine, lead the way," I sigh, pulling off my gloves. I hold them in my hands, leaving the wraps on to cover my knuckles that are scraped up and bloody, and we head upstairs.

My father is sitting in a meeting room with a few of his advisors. Surprise and a hint of pride cross his face when I come in, still recovering my breath from the workout, not nearly enough sweat wiped away with the gym's towel. I smell as bad as those green recruits in the van.

"Vale." His eyebrows are raised so high I hope they don't freeze and stay there. "Enjoying yourself?"

I refuse to react. "Father. It's the middle of the night. What do you need?"

"I need my report," my father says.

"I just got back," I tell him.

"I also came in today. And yet here I am, fulfilling my responsibilities."

I tell him what I know. "The report will come through in the morning. Ten on schedule, one detained at the border. I delivered them to intake about," I check my phone, "three hours ago."

My father and his advisors nod, taking notes.

"There's nothing else?" he asks, an odd question in his voice.

"I'll include as much detail as I can in the report," I tell him, hoping to be back in the shower and in bed as soon as possible. My exhaustion is starting to hit me like a train.

"There was a girl on the train. It sounded like she knew you," my father chooses this moment to tell me.

I can't hide my shock. Truth is, I don't know a lot of girls. Could it be Amity Bloome, with the freckles and the questions?

"Heading here?" I ask.

"Do you want to tell me about her?" He answers my question with his own.

"What did she look like?" I demand. It might not be the same girl.

"Well, I took a picture, of course," my father says smoothly, tapping his phone.

My phone vibrates and I open his message, a photo from the dining car of two people in profile. One in a hoodie, with asymmetrical hair. The other one is Amity but she looks different.

She's wearing street clothes and her long hair has been chopped off and swept up into a short ponytail. It's...cute. She's really...wow, she was pretty in her school uniform but this is something else entirely. I wonder if my dad knows who she is. He wasn't involved with MAV like my mom was, he probably has no idea Amity and I knew each other as kids.

"She talked about you and she asked about a man named Zeph, with red hair."

"One of the new recruits. I'll ask Zeph about this first thing tomorrow," I assure him. "We'll get more answers."

"We will," my father agrees. "I need to know what her deal is, why she followed him up here. Is she working for the PS? Is she some kind of spy?"

"She's a kid," I scoff.

"You're a kid and you're a spy," he growls back.

Well, that might be true. But I've met operatives and Amity was nothing like that. Curious, sure, but not like the battle-hardened women the PS sends up here to the Embassy.

"She says she's on her way up here. If she makes it, she will need to be found. You and Zeph will deal with this and report back to me."

"Yes, sir," I agree.

"And Vale," my father says, his nose wrinkling, "take a shower, buddy."

13

AMITY

AFTER AN ENDLESS TRAIN ride and a stomach-churning few hours in a shabby little plane, Ren brings me to a friend's house. Anchorage is a mix of wide gray roads and crowded back streets filled with houses of all shapes and sizes. There are trucks and wood piles squished into alleys beside ramshackle sheds and mud puddles.

The house is low to the ground and almost rubs up against the neighbors. Unlike the buildings in Canada, this house has windows and peeling green paint. One of the windows is boarded over.

Mobile homes and trailers cluster erratically nearby, some with green lawns flanking them, others on their neighbor's doorstep. There are sheds and cars and bikes and tires everywhere.

Pieces of litter blow along the sidewalk, and graffiti paints the walls. The mountains in the distance are sharp and white-topped against an intensely blue sky.

The early summer air is crisp and bracing. Above us

black birds with red on their wings swirl up into the sky and dive back down, shrieking. The people we see are lean and guarded, mostly men. One guy is walking down the road carrying a baseball bat. He doesn't look like he's going to a game.

We step onto the porch. The door is splashed with streaks of color, a shocking design for a front door. Someone has glued tiny pebbles, shells, and colorful sequins to the surface. Ren knocks. Nothing happens.

Ren knocks again, banging this time.

"Hey, Eli! Open up." We hear steps from inside and the door opens a couple of inches, still locked by a chain.

"Qilan," Ren squeals. The door slams closed, only to open immediately to reveal a tired-looking young woman in jeans with straight dark hair and searching eyes.

"Ren, you made it," she says in a low, rich voice. Her eyes slide to me silently.

"Qilan, this is Ami," Ren introduces me. "She was in the same batch back in the PS."

Qilan nods. "What about—?"

Ren shakes their head. "Yeah, no. I couldn't find him…"

Qilan's lips press together. "I'm sorry," she says finally.

"Can Ami stay here for now? She's looking for a friend and doesn't have a place. She helped me buy my plane ticket from Vancouver!" Ren puts extra pleading in their voice.

Qilan's eyes scan me and she shrugs. "It's okay with me if it's okay with Eli and Moira."

"Great! Come on, kiddo," Ren's enthusiasm knows no bounds. Qilan steps aside and Ren drags me inside calling, "Moira?"

"She'll be back soon," Qilan tells Ren. "She's out collecting. You guys can take the trailer." She adds as an afterthought, "It might be dusty."

"Awesome." Ren grins and Qilan sighs a little. She seems familiar with Ren's enthusiasm.

"Moira put some stuff back there for when you came," Qilan says, offhand, and Ren glances away, blushing. "You should thank her," Qilan tells Ren and she's smiling slightly, like she's teasing Ren.

"Don't worry about me. Go translate something." Ren leads me down a hallway past an open area partially taken up by a piano and sagging couches.

Out back there's an awning and the door to a small, manufactured home. Inside we find a utilitarian kitchen and table and chairs, clean despite Qilan's warning.

Ren smiles, looking around at a few dishes stacked neatly and a note on the counter they grab and read. "Aw, Moira."

I don't know who Moira is but I'd like to find out if there's a shower I can use. Ren opens one door and behind them I see a wide bed with a small pile of clothes folded on it and a desk tucked up to a window overlooking the alley.

Ren sighs deeply. When they turn back I realize they're holding back tears.

"You okay?" I ask.

"I'm happy to be back." Ren sighs. "It's just hard, leaving him behind." They're talking about their brother, I guess. "Next year I'm getting him out no matter what," they murmur.

Ren turns and crosses to another door on the other side of the common area. It's an identical room with a narrow bed. There's a chest of drawers and next to the window is a long, deep table that's covered with oddly shaped cups and vases, along with unrecognizable pottery pieces glazed in different colors.

I turn to Ren. "Is this someone's studio?"

Ren shrugs. "They must have moved on. You can move that stuff back to the main house or take it somewhere, just ask Eli when he gets home."

"It's okay," I respond and check around. The walls are gray and dirty, but the bed is piled with thick blankets.

"This is great, thank you so much, Ren. I really appreciate it."

"No problem, kiddo. I'll arrange it with Eli, no worries. Look, plug your phone into this to charge it," and they show me a port by the bed. "We'll get some clothes that fit you as soon as I catch up with Moira." Ren blushes again.

I raise my eyebrows. "Moira sounds nice."

"Yeah," Ren mumbles. They glance out the window at the bright sunlight. "I have a couple things to do. I'll see you at dinner, okay?"

Ren ducks out, closing my door. I stare at the room. My room in Anchorage. I have a place to sleep. I've got money, and a phone, and a friend. I sit on the edge of the bed and plug my phone in, sending a follow-up message to my mom. I thought she would respond to the message I sent from Kingston, but there's no word back from her. I don't know what time it is in Baltimore.

I leave my phone and go take a shower, determined to smell better even if I have to put the same clothes back on. But by the time I'm out of the shower Ren has come and gone and there's a little pile of pants, shirts, and underwear on my bed. I pull on jeans and a clean T-shirt with a worn sweater that Ren has dug up, or Moira, whoever.

I gather the rest of the clothes off the bed, dropping them into the empty top drawer of the dresser, and lie down after closing the thick window shade which makes the room surprisingly dark.

I don't intend to do more than rest a bit, but I fall so deeply asleep that I wake up with a gasp when there's a sharp knock on the bedroom door and Ren's voice.

"Come on, kiddo, dinner's almost ready."

I take a deep breath. "Okay, I'm coming," I call. I tie my hair back into the still unfamiliar ponytail, quickly reviewing my cover story in my head.

Ren's already on their way out the door to cross into the house and I follow them through. There's a small room in the back of the house with way too many posters, most of them with slogans in red or black ink.

We head into a kitchen with a long table.

Qilan, from earlier, is at the counter, chopping, and next to her is a strikingly pretty girl with red curls and pale skin. She's scraping something out of a bowl into a pan, and she slides it carefully into the oven. I glance at Ren and Ren is staring, looking nervous.

"Hey." Ren's voice croaks and they clear their throat. "How can we help?"

The two at the counter turn.

"Hey, Ren," comes Qilan's rich voice and the girl next to her gives us a wide smile.

She comes over to hug Ren. I turn away as Ren's arms tighten around her and they whisper to each other, the girl's head tilting back for a brief kiss. Ren pulls the girl in close to their side, a grin overtaking their face.

"Ami, this is Moira. Moira, Ami." Moira gives me a friendly nod.

"How'd you get mixed up with this one?" she asks, her voice slightly accented and sly, teasing Ren.

"We met up…" I hesitate, not knowing if I should share the details.

"It was a meet-cute in a holding cell," Ren laughs. "Ami's first time being deported. So adorable!"

Moira shakes her head. "Welcome to Anchorage," she says, deadpan.

Qilan gives me a nod and tilts her head toward the fridge. "When you're done with introductions, could you grate some cheese for us, please?" Qilan drinks from a pretty glass filled with something deep red—maybe wine— and sets the glass down, picking up her knife again.

"Of course," Ren agrees. "Where's Eli?"

"Still out," Moira answers. "Hopefully staying out of trouble this time."

"Eli is an…anarco-communist?" Ren says to me like it's a question.

Qilan snorts. "Libertarian socialist, maybe."

"I believe he's going by post-Marxist anti-capitalist," Moira giggles.

"He'll be back whenever the, um, incident has been resolved," Qilan says with a sigh. "Come on, let's get the cheese going. The cornbread won't take long."

The smell in the kitchen is making my stomach growl audibly. I grate a pile of cheese while Ren pulls plates and silverware out and puts them around the end of the table.

Moira brings the bottle of wine over, then Qilan and Ren dish up chili and cornbread.

Rather than obsess about the details of my backstory, or try to figure out where I can find Zeph tomorrow, I focus on the meal. It's so spicy it makes my eyes water, but in a good way.

APRIL 7, 2018

I read the suggestions in Delegate Ciliberti's op-ed about the tragic Parkland shooting on February 14th ("The real lessons of Parkland shooting"). As a member of Mothers Against Violence, I welcome all ideas for reducing violence.

Unfortunately the plan to add more guns to schools, arming teachers and guards, is not backed up by research. Just look at the recent drop in gun violence in states that have taken MAV's input for new, strict gun license rules. The data shows that fewer guns, not more guns, makes us safer.

The Parkland massacre was the last straw for me, as it was for so many people. In memory of the lives lost, the 28th Amendment was submitted, repealing the 2nd Amendment and the right to bear arms. This new Amendment has already passed both houses of Congress and been ratified by several states, including Maryland.

How will history view the Delegate's words? Will he join the movement to put safety first, to finally reduce the supply of guns in our schools and on our streets? Or will he continue to propose bills that enrich the companies that make and sell guns?

We must pass this Amendment. America needs 38 states to ratify the 28th Amendment and make it the new law of the land. This update to the Constitution will allow for nationwide gun control laws. We will be able to confiscate illegal weapons such as the one used at Parkland. Our children must come first. Sign the Baltimore petition at MAVBaltimore.com.

Sincerely,

Mikayla Adamson

Mothers Against Violence

14

VALE

I WAKE up to yelling in the hallway. That's one thing about this place. Despite the tight control my father and his lieutenants have, there's always something brewing. The raised voices mix with the thud of a body hitting the wall outside my room.

I sigh and turn over, pulling the pillow over my head to block out the yelling. There's louder shouting now, with new voices as guards arrive to break up the fight.

Whatever, I'll get up. I roll over and out of bed and jerk the shade up. It's the same sight I've seen from this window since I moved up here when I was fourteen. Wide blue skies, with white-capped mountains in the distance despite the mild June temperatures. There's a rumble as the train rolls by the school complex that houses the Forge.

I wonder sometimes about the teenagers who walked the halls of this school just ten years ago.

There's no organized school in Anchorage now. People homeschool or move out. Most of the territories accept refugees. Some have stricter rules than others. The strictest rules are in the PS, which is the first thing I need to deal with this morning.

Anchorage is a patchwork of different gangs and militias, with other groups mixed in. There's a whole quarter of artists south of here, and another neighborhood that's mostly First Nations.

We somehow keep the peace between everyone, despite the black-market weapons that find their way up here. The Forge is a big part of that.

It's human nature to fight and win and establish dominance, and that's the best way to keep the peace. A pride of lions is at peace because a leader establishes dominance, protecting the territory and the resources of the pride. Humans are like that also, from what my father says. By protecting the group, being willing to fight and kill, you live as nature intended.

It only breaks down when there's interference in the system, like what they do in the PS. I don't spend much time down there; it's usually a quick in and out with the new recruits. Now I've got this loose end, Calista Bloome's daughter out of the PS, possibly on her way up here following her friend.

I'll need to go down and find Zeph, find out more about Amity and see if there are any leads on her location. If she's joined up with another group, well, that might be out of our control.

For some reason the thought of her with a rival militia, cozying up to the Brotherhood, has my stomach turning. There's no reason for her to be anywhere but here, even if she is a spy. Keep your friends close and your enemies closer, as they say.

My brain conjures an image of holding her close, my arms wrapped around her, laying her head on my shoulder. I could protect her. Anchorage is not like the PS. She'll need someone. It could be me.

Down in the cafeteria there's a low murmur of voices but it's fairly quiet, even with all the men here. A lot of the work we do is outside. It's physical, and the guys are hungry. I get a tray of eggs and potatoes and wander the large hall, searching for this guy Zeph.

I see red hair in the far corner and head over. It's a table of new recruits and Zeph is sitting near the end. I slide in beside him and he nods in greeting. Like all these guys, he looks nervous. I eat a little and then I'm direct with him.

"Tell me about the girl you were with at the courthouse."

Zeph starts. His face clouds with confusion. "She's nothing. A friend."

"Is she your girlfriend?" I ask, feeling tense.

"No, nothing like that."

I wait, silent.

"I'm not, she's not my—well, I'm gay," he tells me.

I nod, relaxing, something like relief sweeping over me. "What's her name?"

He hesitates. I wait for his answer. I already know the words but hearing them come out of his mouth feels exciting, somehow, and like a complication.

"Amity Bloome. Her mom is a big MAV leader."

I know that, of course. But I don't remember this guy from that MAV group. He must have met her after the Integration. "So you're friends. Was she also interested in leaving the PS? Involved with rebels?"

Zeph laughs. "Amity is, like, a poster child for the PS. She understands there are problems, but she thinks she can change them from the inside. Yeah, right," he adds, more to himself. "I think she was going up for HighClear actually, that's what she said."

HighClear, that's interesting. She would have gone off to the Institute with the other soldiers in training.

"From what I know," he hedges.

"Any chance she could have been deported?" I ask.

Zeph laughs again. "Amity? No way. She's barely been out of Baltimore."

"Could she be following you—trying to catch up with you?" I ask him.

Zeph hesitates, considering. "She's...loyal. And I think —worried about me. I did sort of ask her about refusing the Oath and coming along...but no." He shakes his head. "She wouldn't."

"She was spotted on a depo train in New York," I tell him, finally getting to the point.

"Amity Bloome?" Zeph's surprise is so genuine I can't imagine he's faking it. This guy is still a baby, refused his Oath just a few days ago.

"You just said you suggested she refuse her Oath. Is it so unbelievable that she did?"

"Amity is..." His face softens. "Dedicated. Maybe she changed her mind," but skepticism clouds it again. "But she's so innocent. I told you, she wouldn't last a minute on her own."

The anxiety that has been plaguing me deepens. "But she was there, on the train. She came to the Forge car, and bought a phone under the table."

"That couldn't be her." He shakes his head again.

I pull up the picture on my phone. Zeph's eyes bug out, and he holds it close to his face.

"Yeah, that's her. Aw, her hair." He's sad, but long hair is pretty much a symbol of matriarchal oppression down there. "She cut her hair."

"Yeah, man. She cut her hair, she got herself a phone, and she was asking about you. Did you tell her you were coming to Anchorage specifically? Did you talk about our group?"

He thinks. "I might have mentioned it. I trust her."

"Could the PS have sent her?" I ask. "Could she be spying for them?"

"Amity? No offense, but she would make a terrible spy."

"Well," I grit my teeth. "We're trying to locate her in Anchorage now."

Zeph stiffens. "She's in the city? Alone?"

"She was traveling with someone, another deportee, from what they said," I tell him.

"God, Amity."

"You're the one who suggested she come," I say, annoyed that he's acting so worried that she apparently took his advice.

He sighs. "I didn't think it through. Is she going to be safe?" he asks. "Can you find her?"

"Yeah, we're gonna find her. Do you have any idea where she would go? Who she could be with?"

He shakes his head slowly. I'm tired of this guy already.

"I've known Amity forever, she's...really naïve."

"Okay, you've got nothing to go on. I'm going to find her, and we'll touch base about this again. Everything you just said better be the truth. And if she is undercover for the PS it's a situation that will need to be...handled."

Zeph's eyes shoot to the side and he says nothing. I shove my chair back and drop my empty tray off at the kitchen before heading to one of the storage rooms.

Not everything around here runs smoothly, but the rooms where we store weapons and supplies are kept in order by the guys who are ex-military. They're pretty good at that sort of thing.

I'm going to start down at the market. Show her picture around, see if anyone's seen her. I don't need to be heavily armed, but I still grab a Glock and holster, pulling a jacket over top. I sign out the ammo, chatting with the guy on duty, and load the gun up.

I have my phone. I have cash left from the trip. The market is down on Spenard, and I can walk there. It will give me a chance to get out of this building.

I grab my baseball hat on the way out and pull it down low, giving me cover. I don't stick out too much, but people recognize me as Isaiah Adamson's kid and I don't want word to leak out that the Forge is after this girl in case it scares her away.

I'm ready. I head down one more hallway, pushing the metal door open into the blinding sunlight, and walk down the road to the market.

15

VALE

I WAS GONE for a couple weeks, working on this latest run, and spring has finally taken hold in Anchorage. It feels good, the heat of the sun on my skin. My mom would have hated it up here, she loved warm weather. Even Maryland in winter was too cold for her, she always wanted to flee to Texas and visit her family for long stretches in January.

The people around me look a little desperate, but not more than usual. I feel bad for the homeschooled kids up here, who get whatever education their parents can scrounge up.

I thought the Forge could organize a school, but I don't think that's going to happen. We've contributed, we've helped keep the peace, but now my dad has bigger plans, and they don't involve school.

"Vale," says a man behind me in a voice I don't recognize.

I turn slowly, not in a rush, but wary. It's a guy my age

from the Forge. He's been here almost as long as I have, dragged by his father. I try to remember his name.

"Vale, how's it going?" he asks, hurrying to catch up.

I nod, giving him a curt "Good" and wondering how to keep this interaction as short as possible. I don't know him, and I'm not interested in changing that.

"I'm on a supply run," he volunteers. I glance over and he looks happy, excited.

"For what?" I ask.

"Another bike," he tells me, his voice vibrating with excitement.

"Nice," I allow. Now I remember, this guy is super into motorcycles.

There's an awkward pause while I wait for him to leave.

"What…what are you up to?" he asks.

I guess I was supposed to volunteer that information.

I sigh. I'm not telling this guy anything about Amity. Frankly, I don't want any of the guys at the Forge to see her or know about her. The silence is awkward while I self-reflect about why I'm so protective of her.

Probably stuff I was brainwashed with as a kid, about protecting women and all that. What a crock. We found out how that worked out. The minute they got a little power they ran rampant with it, at least in the PS.

"Uh…" the guy says. "I guess this is me."

Oh, he's still here. He peels off down a side street to a place that works on cars and bikes, all kinds of vehicles. I keep my stride steady.

I'm almost to the market now. I want to look confident, like I have a clear purpose for being here. The market brings together a lot of different kinds of people.

Sometimes that works out fine, but sometimes there are disagreements and fights.

I sweep the entrance with my eyes. A leaning sign jammed into the rough ground next to the parking lot says "Spenard Market." Then it's rows of haphazard tables and pop-up tents.

I'll pick up something to eat where I can take a look around. With that decision I stride past people selling art and clothing and bread and vegetables and get to another reason I came down here.

"Back safe?" a warm voice inquires. Mrs. Perez is manning the register of the empanada stand, while her nieces and nephews scurry around filling orders.

"Got back last night," I say, my eyes darting to hers for a quick smile and then continuing to scan the market.

"Two chicken empanadas?" she asks, starting to reach into the case with a napkin.

"Just one," I correct gently.

She pouts and I hurry to add, "I'm coming from breakfast."

"Forge food," she grumbles and I can't escape a warm feeling, a throwback to my days in Baltimore with my mom. I don't complain about Mrs. Perez trying to feed me well. She's a bright spot in an existence that doesn't have too many.

"Okay, one," she agrees and hands it over the register. I reach for cash to pay her but she refuses, pushing my hand back. "Welcome home."

"Mrs. Perez...I, come on." I urge her to take it.

"Not today, Vale Adamson," she sings and turns away. I tuck the bill in the tip jar and slouch around the side of the stand, scanning the crowded market for Amity.

I'm on Forge business, to find out more about her, but the mission feels a little more personal than that. My eye finally catches on brown wavy hair on a tall girl near the entrance.

I don't move right away, just clock her and wait for the girl to turn so I can see if it's her. Something about the way she walks, a little unsure, standing straight as a rod, like she's forcing herself to appear brave and confident, makes me think I found her.

Frustratingly, she doesn't turn so I push off where I'm leaning, finishing the end of the empanada and throwing the wrapper in the trash, and push through the crowd. I keep the wavy hair in my line of sight, but with space between us, in case she turns around.

Then the girl gets in line at the coffee truck and turns a little, and it's Amity.

My foot takes a step toward her before I catch myself and slink back. I see it's her now, her flashing eyes and pretty, freckled face. I need to hold back and assess more before I talk to her. My eyes wander down her body. She's wearing tight jeans that hug her long legs, and a leather jacket with a knit cap pulled over her shorter hair.

As she waits in line, she's talking to someone. The man in front of her turns, and I tense, but he's laughing at something she said and answering her back. I don't trust him.

Once she has her coffee she clutches it in her hands, inhaling deeply with her eyes closed over the cup. I instinctively breathe in with her, then catch myself. Weird

PS stuff, to match your breathing to other people. I hate that they're in my head.

Now she walks a little slower, not wanting to spill, drinking her coffee as she takes in the market. The smart thing would be to follow her from a distance, then I'd learn where she's staying, which would tell us a lot.

But I'm not leaving without talking to her. I want her to laugh like that for me, look in my eyes while she says something, anything. I continue to trail her, wondering what she's after, meditating on the way she walks and what happened to all her hair, until she stops in the last place I expected. Directly in front of the knife dealer.

BALTIMORE SUN *READERS RESPOND*

MARCH 13, 2019

Mothers Against Violence welcomes the new head of the Baltimore Police Department ("Vivian Thomas sworn in as Baltimore's 41st police commissioner"). This is the first time that peace groups in the city, led by Mothers Against Violence, have been included in choosing a Police Commissioner.

Ms. Thomas made it clear to MAV that her priority is making Baltimore safer now and in the future. She's expressed full support for MAV in the city, and she supports the key pillars of MAV's approach: regulation, liability, and confiscation.

Regulation of guns has had a dramatic effect, with shootings and murders down sharply for a third year in a row. This February was the first month to be totally free of gun violence—no shootings reported in the city for the entire month.

With liability laws now updated, gun makers and sellers are finally responsible for injuries and deaths caused by the machinery they produce and sell. There is a simple guideline: did a gun pass through your hands and go on to kill someone? You will be sued and held liable.

MAV supports a carrot-and-stick approach to gun confiscation. Generous gun buybacks, along with collecting guns that don't meet safety standards, will be a priority of Ms. Thomas. Sign up for the MAV gun buyback program and receive up to $5,000, details at MAVBaltimore.com.

Sincerely,
Mikayla Adamson
Mothers Against Violence

16

AMITY

EARLIER THAT MORNING

I WAKE up to a motor revving outside and it's so loud. The e-cars back home don't make a lot of noise, but there sure are a lot of noisy cars up here, and trucks, and other kinds of vehicles.

I do my Twenty this morning, even though my mom's not here to remind me. I know I don't have to, I'm not wearing a SafeGuard, the Society will never know. But it felt weird on the train, skipping it. Not that I wanted to do it in front of everyone.

The twenty minutes of meditation center me. I need it more than I realized. I feel like myself again. My emotions aren't a cloudy haze; I can see them in front of me, name them, and put them aside as needed.

I make the bed and linger before the dresser, staring at the clothes and trying to decide what to wear. I wish they were all the same like at home, it makes it much easier.

Then my phone beeps so I quickly throw on a steel-gray T-shirt with flames on the front and a pair of worn black jeans and bring the phone over to the table, pulling on my jacket. It's pretty chilly, even with the heater I can hear running in the middle room.

I understand the phone better now and I can go into the program the PS is using to communicate with me. It doesn't come online every time I try it—the reception must be intermittent.

There's a message for me from "mom", at least that's what it says. I don't know who's on the other side of the text for sure.

> Hi Ami how are you doing?

I write back.

> Fine, I'm staying with friends. They are nice.

> That's great honey.

I blink at the phone. I can't imagine my mom using the word honey.

> Still looking for your friend?

> Yes

I assume they mean Zeph.

> Do you think he's at the Forge?

> I guess so. I'm going to look for him today.

Ok, let me know how it goes. Stay safe.

Even if it isn't my mom, it's still comforting to know they're keeping track of me. There's GPS in my watch and depending on the signal they can probably track me that way also. I don't know if it's sending them all my bio info like the SafeGuards do.

I decide to look for tea and something to eat. I dig around and find a knit hat for the chill.

In the main house Qilan is at the table, with papers and a tattered book. She has a cup that's steaming.

"Hey, Ami," she greets me quietly. "That water's hot, help yourself to breakfast. I think Ren's out with Moira."

I gratefully take a look and they have a collection of jars with all kinds of herbs and even black tea. I consider it nervously. The caffeine in the coffee was enough excitement for now, I decide, and make myself tea with peppermint leaf. There's bread sitting out here so I toast it and spread it with something from a jar in the fridge that says butter and take a bite standing at the counter. It tastes like apples, and it's delicious.

"Thank you," I say quietly, not wanting to disturb Qilan's work. "Can I contribute some money for the...food and stuff?"

She focuses a few more seconds before looking up. "That would be great. Catch up with Eli about it, okay?"

"Sure. Is he here?"

Qilan shakes her head. "He's out again." Her eyes skim over to a pile of flyers on the counter. *What lessons can communal-utopians learn from libertarian theories of trust?* is written at the top.

"Okay," I agree.

I bring my tea over timidly, but she gives a friendly nod to the chair next to her. Qilan continues reading her book quietly, making notes in her notebook as she goes. I don't recognize the language she's reading.

I munch on my toast and sit in silence, watching her read.

I think about trying to find Zeph. I have no idea where to start looking for one guy in this whole city. Maybe I can start with finding the Forge, since that should be easier to locate. I think of the cold stare of Isaiah Adamson telling me he'd see me in Anchorage with a shiver. Maybe he will.

And maybe I'll see Vale again. Vale was nothing like his dad. Was the placid guard demeanor an act, or is that what he's like now?

"There's a group, a place I'm looking for," I say when Qilan shuts her notebook and takes a sip of tea. "It's called the Forge."

Qilan shakes her head no, a quick shake. I watch her carefully, noting a slight twitch of her right eye. Her breathing stays slow and deep.

She turns toward me. "Ami," she says. "Do you know what the Forge is?"

"A rebel group," I say, "and my friend Zeph might be there. I'm trying to find him."

"It's a militia," Qilan corrects me, and this time she cringes more visibly. "It's hundreds," she says, "thousands of men in a big compound together. They've got weapons, and money. Can you imagine what that's like? How old are you, Ami?"

"Eighteen," I tell her. "I've been to fights back in the PS," I lie, using the nickname everyone seems to call it up here.

"This is different," she says. "There's no police. No PS soldiers. The Forge, the Brotherhood, they do whatever they want. We're pretty safe down here in Spenard, they leave the artists alone. But if you go there—some of them hate women," she says more quietly. "For starting MAV, for the Universal Accord and the Integration, and, you know..." She trails off.

"What?" I ask.

"You're very pretty," she says, her eyes sweeping me. "Young and pretty, and there aren't a lot of women in Anchorage. You'd be putting yourself in a lot of danger. I don't leave Spenard without Eli," she admits.

Wow, okay. So this is what my mother was saying, about being careful and defending myself. I need to learn some defense skills. I'll get a weapon, and then I'll look for Zeph.

"So what do I need, a gun? A knife? Where can I get one?"

Qilan raises her eyebrows. "Slow down, sister. You can get something at the market, and Eli or Ren can show you how to use it, okay? It's not as easy as it sounds, threatening people, hurting them."

She looks skeptical. I don't see the problem. This is what they will teach me at the Institute: how to use Tasers and stun batons. How to control and threaten when needed for the Society and the public good. This is like HighClear training, just with different weapons.

Qilan tells me where the market is and I tie on my boots.

"Here, give me your phone," she says.

I hand it to her.

She types and hands it back to me. "My number is in there now, call me if you need anything. And stay in the neighborhood today, no matter what you hear about your friend, okay?"

"Got it. Thank you," I tell her.

I walk down through the alley. It's still early in the morning but the sun is high in the sky and blindingly bright. It's so beautiful up here. I'm not used to seeing the jagged mountains in the distance. The street I walk down has the same jumble of houses and trailers and tiny shops squeezed in here and there. In a large parking lot the market stretches out across the street.

White pop-up tents litter the area in lurching rows. People are clustered in groups and waiting in lines. I explore the market for a little while before I smell hot, fragrant coffee coming from a truck that's set up at the end of a row. Without thinking my feet bring me to the end of the line, my resolution to avoid caffeine discarded already. I'll get coffee first, then explore the market more.

I chat a little with the other people in line before I remember that this isn't Baltimore, and I can't let my guard down. My phone and money are in an inner pocket of my black leather coat, and I pull my knit hat down over my hair which skims my shoulders, tickling my neck, so different from my heavy braid.

The man at the coffee truck makes me a cup of coffee without looking at me. He's engrossed in a conversation with a friend about something that happened at the Brotherhood last week. Their voices rise to a shout, arguing about "whose mess it is." I try not to cringe at the sound of raised voices as I turn away and let the cup of coffee warm my hands.

I explore the aisles. There is a table piled with mushrooms. Someone else has a cooler and no sign of what's in it. There are sad vegetables next to stands piled with worn plates and cups and one with aging rugs. There's a lot of art vendors, selling all sorts of paintings and statues. I see why this is the market for the arts neighborhood.

There's even a young man passing out flyers that look like the ones back in the kitchen. I wonder if it's Eli but I hear him talking to someone and he says he's from out of the city.

Finally at the end of the row I spot a tent with a different product. Lined up on the table are the shining blades of several knives. I pause in front, blinking at the knives and collecting my thoughts for what to say, when I feel someone standing close behind me.

17

AMITY

WHEN I WAS in middle school, back when the security stations were still used for security and not just for watching us all the time, there was a time I had to use one.

My mom taught me what to do if I was ever scared or saw violence. I should press the call button on the nearest station and CSOs would come right away. In school we did simulations.

But this wasn't a simulation. I was in the next neighborhood over, Homewood, hanging out with girls from school. I can't remember what we were doing, probably sitting around talking. I was twelve.

There must have been yelling in one of the houses because I remember we fell silent, listening. My brain told me that something was wrong. It was quiet as I looked around the neighborhood. Then with a bang, a screen door slammed and a woman ran out of her house. She was in bare feet and she ran into the yard and paused for a moment.

Everyone stopped to watch her. Her panic, the tight energy of her desperation, drew my gaze. The trees, the grass, the sun, my friends stopped as she froze, seemingly trying to make up her mind.

While we watched her, a man came silently around the corner of the house from the side. He was tall, and I remember the boots he was wearing, black and thick-soled.

He grabbed her roughly, and my heart hammered, adrenaline flooding my system. There was a collective gasp as my friend grabbed my hand and we sat, petrified, under a tree across the street as the woman silently struggled in his grasp and the man slowly dragged her back toward the front door.

I waited with wide eyes for someone to do something. For one of the girls to get up and tell someone, go and find help.

I could see the security station a few houses down and my eyes darted back and forth, looking to see if he was watching us, judging how far the button was and how long it would take for me to run there.

The woman did something, pushed him, broke his grasp, and the struggle renewed on the doorstep. My legs straightened. I don't remember deciding, but I was running down the street. It took forever to get there. Each step, lifting from the ground, a slow arc through the air, and another push off the ground as my sneakers hit the pavement.

I felt the attention of the two grown-ups snap to me but before they could do anything I was there, pressing the button. I huddled against the station as if it could keep me safe and the other girls ran to cluster around the camera, the microphones, and the blue button to call the Security Officers.

After that everything happened too rapidly for me to digest. The man was yanking her inside the house and slamming the door just as white vans were speeding down the street toward us. My friends pointed to the house and the CSOs clustered in front of the door.

"He won't let them in," a girl gasped to me in horror just as the tall woman in front raised her foot, encased in a heavy gray boot, and kicked the door in. The officers swarmed into the house, Tasers in hand.

While we waited, breathless, for evidence that the woman was okay, that the Security Officers had caught the Oath Breaker, I felt someone standing behind me. Whether I could see the edge of her pale gray boots or not, I knew it was an Officer. She stood directly behind me, protecting me, protecting all of us.

I had done my best, I had played my part, and I could relax now. The woman behind me radiated power and calm; she would take care of everything. I was safe.

The memory flashes through my mind as I force my eyes to trace the bright, sharp edges of the knives on the table in front of me despite feeling someone standing directly behind me. They stand close, closer than a stranger should stand.

And there they stay. Regulating my breathing, I glance down. I see black boots and jeans. From the corners of my eyes, side to side, there's nothing. When I raise my eyes to the vendor he has busied himself organizing sheaths and is avoiding looking at me. Me and whoever is behind me.

I'm frozen in time again, unwilling to break the silence, not ready to turn around and start an interaction. It's him —the scent of pine and soap and the hint of chlorine is exactly the same.

From above my left ear, a low murmur. "What are you up to, Pepper?"

I wait three beats before turning and guardedly glance up. Vale, the confusing grown-up version of the boy I remember, is here, standing less than a foot from me. He's wearing what is apparently Alaska standard, jeans and a leather jacket, with a baseball hat pulled low. His eyes are swathed in shadow.

Instead of answering him, I drink in what I can without running my gaze up and down his body. The broad shoulders, the wide brown curve of his neck, the clean-shaven jaw and full lips.

I freeze. My brain is trying to remind me that this man is part of a dangerous militia, that he stole Zeph away and the Society has put me in charge of spying on him and the Forge. The memory of his father still curls around my subconscious, cold and deadly.

But his broad body, standing so close to me, shielding me from the rest of the market, is giving me the same safe, grounded feeling that the Security Officer did in my friend's yard all those years ago. I'm relaxing, I'm softening, and suddenly it's easier to talk to him.

"Sorry, have we met?" I try out, repressing a smile. He blows an exasperated breath.

"Come on. What are you doing *here*?" he demands, glancing back to the knife dealer. One hand comes to my back lightly and I close my eyes, feeling the brush of his fingers like a siren going off.

"I need to talk to you, Amity," he whispers in my ear.

I shoot him an alarmed glance and turn back to the knives.

"How much for this one?" I ask the vendor sweetly. He seems frozen and doesn't answer me right away, flicking a worried glance at Vale. The pressure of Vale's hand on my back increases as he turns me firmly toward an alley and ushers me away from the weapons vendor and a few yards from the crowded crush of the market.

Vale looks around nervously and then at me, gauging how I'm reacting. It's kind of funny how nervous he seems.

"You okay there, Vale? I'll protect you. Are these artists freaking you out?" I ask.

At the mention of his name his attention snaps back on me like a warm light.

"Who told you my name?"

I raise my eyebrows in response. "I remember you," I tell him quietly.

He's tucked us against the brick wall of an alley. There's garbage trampled down in layers underfoot, nothing like the sparkling alleys of Baltimore.

"Tell me what you're doing in Anchorage," he orders, staring down at me intently.

"Looking for Zeph. Is he at the Forge?" I take a gamble, trying to act like I know more than I do.

"Your mother is Calista Bloome and I know you were up for HighClear. How did you end up here?"

"I got deported, didn't I?" I go for flippant.

I think it works, because Vale's brown eyes widen. Just as I think he is going to answer me there's a commotion back in the market. A vendor is upset, and shouting at another man. People are jumping in to yell and push each other.

I twist around to see what's happening just as a loud crack echoes and Vale's touching me again, turning us and pulling us down, tucking me against him. The shouting grows louder as a fight breaks out and there's a loud pop, pop. Is someone shooting a gun?

I try to see around him but Vale's arm keeps me down, against him, his body blocking me from whatever is happening at the market. It doesn't sound good. Vale seems to agree. With my head against the smooth leather of his jacket, his body warmth seeping through, I can feel his heart rate increase and his breathing speed up.

"We need to get out of here," he tells me, low and urgent. I wiggle against his grasp while he's reaching inside his coat.

"Amity, what are you doing?" he demands.

"I'm getting out of here," I tell him and break his grasp on my arm. "And don't call me that, call me Ami."

"Where can I find you?" he asks, following me up the alley. I pull my hat down and slip away further, edging around the crowd toward the other side of the market.

"I'll meet you back here," I tell him with a small smile. Vale's head turns as that worried energy comes back. I see the street I came on and slip further away from him. *Tomorrow*, I mouth at him, *meet you here tomorrow*.

He nods, standing still and letting me go. The people

swirl around him, men, some women, fleeing the market, trying to get away from the fight.

I can still see him when I glance back, rooted to the spot where I left him, his head turned toward me. I can't see his eyes under the shade of his hat, but I feel his attention on me, watching me.

18

AMITY

THE NEXT MORNING Qilan hands me a shopping list. It's written on a scrap of paper ripped out of her notebook. On the back are notes in the language she's studying, Dena'ina.

I scan the list. I saw most of this stuff when I was at the market yesterday, before the excitement. I pull on my jacket and check that I have cash.

Qilan still looks a little concerned, maybe because of my report of what happened yesterday with the fight breaking out.

"Ami, just so you know, you don't have to go back there. You can take it easy, get used to things up here." Underneath her initial suspicion she's kind of a motherly person. I saw that last night when she was talking with Ren in a low voice about Ren's brother. She went out late with Ren to "get Eli out of a jam." Now she's given me something to do, some way to help, which I appreciate, so I tell her that.

"I'm happy to have something to do, Qilan. I'm used to having a lot going on." I'm a little surprised I don't feel more scared. But the market's not that far, and even without security stations or CSOs nearby, I feel like I can watch for danger and get back to the house quickly if I need to.

"I've got this. I'll call if I have any questions or if I need anything," I assure her.

"Okay," she agrees and turns back to her work. The feeling of her trusting me, believing I can keep myself safe and get what the house needs, warms my heart.

It's sunny again today, and a little warmer. I keep my coat on, since it feels a little bit like protection, but unzip to cool off. Near the market I start to sharpen my gaze, scanning a little more carefully. I'm watching for people in an argument or anyone carrying a weapon. Also, if Vale is here, I'd prefer to see him before he sneaks up on me again.

With that in mind, I skim the outside of the market, staying close to the clumps of people, mimicking them, trying to blend in. I see a couple of tall men, but no Vale.

I slip in from the side, away from the main entrance, and wait for coffee, surreptitiously glancing around me. I still don't see him. Clutching my cup of coffee, I retreat back to the edge, relaxing my gaze, letting my attention flit from one thing to another.

I know eventually I'll have to start collecting the things on Qilan's list, but there's not a huge rush. I've got all morning.

Then I catch a flash of someone, standing over by the knife dealer from yesterday. Close cropped hair and a body and shoulders a little taller and broader than the men around him.

I slip over to the left, lingering behind a line of people waiting for the fishmonger. The smell of fish is strong and I breathe through my mouth for a minute while I wait for him to move on.

Vale walks slowly down the next aisle of tables and tents, his head a slow swivel from side to side. I can't keep a small smile off my face, thinking he might be looking for me but I found him first.

I stay behind. My guess is that he will turn the corner and go down the next aisle, checking all the people in that direction.

I'm a little surprised when he jerks open a tattered door and strides into a building at the edge of the market. It has a broad window in the front with a counter and stools. I shrink back, peeking out from behind a parked truck.

Then I glance around. I'm not sure how weird I'm acting, but no one seems to be paying attention.

I watch through the window as Vale grabs a drink—is that alcohol? I can't tell—and settles down at the counter, all the way to the side where a shadow partially hides him from view. He's looking out at the market.

I smile. It's a good idea, watching from the window. He didn't realize I would be here before him. I duck over to the side of the building, wondering if there's an entrance in the back. Behind the row of joined buildings is a parking lot and dumpster, trash strewn around, and back doors to the shops.

For some reason my heart is beating faster, the nerves I

expected before I came to the market catching up with me a little late.

Giving myself a shake, I jerk the back door open and stride through. A little bell rings—darn it—and I see several heads turn, including the bartender and a couple of men hunched over pints in the middle of the morning. Weird.

Vale's head turns too.

I give him a feigned look of surprise and then proceed to ignore him as best I can while I approach the bar.

When the bartender looks up to help me I freeze, looking around. There's no alcohol in the Peaceful Society, and I don't want to drink any now. But all I see scribbled on the board and lined up behind this bar are different kinds of bottles and alcoholic drinks.

"What will it be?" the man asks.

I open my mouth and close it. Should I get a beer and not drink it? I feel myself starting to flush, embarrassed as I search for an answer to his question.

"She'll have a Shirley Temple." Vale's snuck up, taking advantage of my inability to place a drink order.

I furrow my brow at him but he mutters "It's non-alcoholic" as the man turns away to mix some things together in a glass, topped off with a cherry. Vale draws a bill out to pay for it before I can object.

"Hey, I got it," I say, but the bartender takes the money from Vale, handing me the drink with a shrug.

Deep sigh. My dream of sidling up to him at the counter with a nonchalant "hey" is dashed as he leads me over and waits while I plop down on the stool next to him with a little huff.

He seems to be suppressing a grin as he slides onto his stool. "Did I ruin your entrance?"

"Did you find what you're looking for?" I ask archly, tilting my head to indicate the large window showing a view of the market. Vale's eyes dart to the back door and he shrugs.

"Okay, you're sneaky," he allows.

"Thank you! Very sneaky, just remember that," I agree.

He stares at me, still with that shadow of a smile on his face.

"What?" I demand.

"I'm surprised you came back after yesterday. Fights, gunshots…"

"Hey," I bristle. "I said I'd meet you. I'm not afraid of that stuff…"

He arches an eyebrow at me.

"Get out of here," I mutter. "You came back, too. Don't you have other stuff to do?"

"My stuff is here," he says. "This is Anchorage, the town where I live."

"The town where you hang out at a bar," I glance at my e-watch, "at ten a.m. on a Thursday?"

"Yes, absolutely," he says but his eyes are laughing at me.

When he was a kid he was hard to play with. One of those kids who doesn't always relate. A little too well-spoken, his humor a little too dry to fit in.

I shake my head. "You haven't changed much, have you?"

Vale looks down at himself. "Is that so? Exactly the same, huh?"

I huff. "That's not what I meant. You're still...apart from everyone, sort of," I hedge, not liking how it sounds.

His gaze softens. "Not from you, Ami."

I remember that too. The careful way he treated me.

His eyes are warm. "You've changed a lot."

I narrow my eyes, waiting for a leer, but his gaze is hot and glued to my face. I catch my breath.

"In what way, Vale?" I ask and his lips press together when I say his name. He seems to struggle inwardly for a moment, then he glances away and the intensity of our eye contact is broken.

"I never expected you here, of all places. Thought you were PS forever," he tells me.

"PS?" I ask.

"Peaceful Society." He says it with a grimace like it's distasteful.

I blink, not sure what to say. "What about you? Where did you go?" I ask him.

"My dad moved up here," he answers shortly. "I came with him."

"What about your mom?" What happened to the woman I remember, my mom's friend in Mothers Against Violence?

His gaze drops. When he looks up, it's with tight formality. "My mom died."

"Oh, Vale, I'm sorry."

Abruptly he hops off his stool. I blink and he clears his throat.

"Come on," he directs me. He's lost me with this quick turnabout.

"Come where?" I ask.

"You're shopping, right? At the market? I'll come with you."

"You don't need to do that," I murmur, stepping down off my stool as well.

"You can tell me all about what you're doing up here."

I roll my eyes at him. "*You* can tell me about the Forge and what's happening with Zeph."

He frowns. Somehow, without planning to, I follow him out the front door into the bright sunlight.

"Well?" he demands.

Gosh, it will be like shopping with a bodyguard. I swallow and pull the list out of my pocket.

"Potatoes?" I offer weakly, and he steers me toward a vegetable seller.

"This guy's potatoes are fresh, usually the best," he says, and despite myself I grin and relax a little. Vale's keeping a lookout. He'll help me get the right things for Qilan.

I'm grateful. That must be this warm feeling inside me.

AUGUST 23, 2019

Hooray for the successful rescue of 12 boys and their coach from a cave system in Northern Thailand ("'Everyone is safe': Daring rescue saves all 12 boys and their coach from flooded cave in Thailand"). What an amazing way for private, public, and government groups to work together to save lives.

Here in America we have our own chance for the government, companies, and citizens to come together to save lives. The brand-new 28th Amendment to the constitution, repealing the right to own a gun, gives us that chance.

Congress must pass the new gun laws that have been working already in many states. People will no longer need to worry that in some states a person on the street could be legally walking around with a loaded gun.

Let's move quickly, just as the rescuers did in the cave rescue. Their lives were in danger, and there are many lives in the US that are in danger from guns every day. We can make our own daring rescue by outlawing semi-automatic weapons and banning public carry. Let Congress hear your voice on Labor Day at the National Mall.

Sincerely,
Mikayla Adamson
Mothers Against Violence

19

VALE

IT GOES ON FOR DAYS. My father breathing down my neck for more information about Amity. Her friend Zeph bugging me, worried sick. I can't convince her to do more than shop together at the market.

She's naturally slippery, not what I would expect from someone raised in the PS. She wears something different every day, but blends in with the people around her. A slim gray hoodie. A canvas coat. On a warmer day a tank top carelessly hugs her body.

She's stronger than I thought, her muscles wiry. I try not to stare. My first impression of her in the courthouse, scanning her wrist, I remember reaching down, but she's pretty tall. And she can look commanding when she sets her shoulders, pulls her face into that PS mask, and sets off through the market.

Ami's careless about her safety, making small talk with men I avoid, stopping to chat with teenagers lounging around the entrance. When we talk, she asks about her friend.

"Is Zeph okay, can I see him?"

"He's fine, and no. It's not going to change," I say curtly the third time she asks on a cloudy, humid day.

The world is tinged gray and Ami's wearing a fraying leather jacket today over a black T-shirt. Her brown wavy hair is pulled back tight into a ponytail.

"Can you..." The usual frustration crosses her face. "Vale, please just tell me what to do. I need a chance to speak with him. Can I at least get his phone number?" she pleads.

I don't like saying no to her, despite the amount of practice I have by now. She keeps demanding I take her to the Forge in the same careless way she chats up the weapons dealer, who she should definitely be avoiding.

She's got an air of innocence, or she's pulling the wool over my eyes. Innocence can resemble fearlessness, and that's how she comes off, teetering on the line in between. I see the looks of respect she gets in the market now. She shows up each day, talks to everyone, drinks her coffee, and picks up the food she takes back to wherever she's staying.

Sometimes I find her by the farm stands, picking through buckets of asparagus and strawberries. Other times she's by the woman selling shoes or in line for coffee. I stay with her until she slips away, still refusing to let me go with her.

I could follow her, of course. I *should* follow her with all the pressure on me to find out more about Amity Bloome, but for some reason I want her to trust me.

"Haven't your...roommates," I stumble over the words, "told you about the Forge?"

Ami gives that shrug, the one that could be careless or thoughtless or just a willingness to put herself in danger. Zeph says it's because she doesn't know any better and I worry that he's right.

"Vale." She leans lightly against me as we wait in the crowded line for coffee and I immediately relax. Is she doing this to me intentionally? "It's not just Zeph. If I'm going to live up here I need to learn to defend myself."

"Your roommates aren't helping with that?"

She huffs. "They would, but they're painting and writing all the time."

"You certainly act like you can defend yourself," I lean down to say in her ear. A shiver goes through her but she doesn't put another inch between us.

"Just a front," she whispers back, looking up at me through half-closed eyes. "Don't tell me you're falling for it too, *Your Majesty*."

I cringe. "Don't call me that," I snap. Sometimes men call my father King, but I hate that.

"I see the way they treat you," she says slyly, turning the conversation away from herself. "I see how they stare at you. You're practically a prince around here."

I turn away from her, in time to see several people quickly point their eyes to the ground. Okay, yeah.

"It's not me," I murmur back. "It's my father." Taking a chance, I tell her, "He wants to meet you...again."

She swallows, and this time she looks worried. Good. Fear of my father is a healthy reaction.

"Why?" she asks.

We get to the front of the line. I buy us coffees and don't miss the pleasure flickering across her face as she draws a deep breath of the steam coming off it, cuddling the cup to her chest.

"There's nothing in it for you, I assure you," I answer. "He probably wants to use you for the Forge." I'm not sure why I'm telling her this. "Thinks he can get to the PS through you."

"Maybe he can," she says and keeps her gaze steady. We've slipped down into the alley, away from the crowd. When she says stuff like this I don't know what to think. Is she really a deportee? Does she want to help the Forge or hurt it? She's playing a dangerous game.

I don't honestly care that much about my father's organization. I have to serve him, serve his lieutenants, so I do it well and keep my place in the hierarchy. But frankly it seems just as corrupt as the PS and that corporation that runs Canada.

"Vale." Ami lifts her head, and her deep blue eyes meet mine. I like the way she says my name, the A high and wide before she slips into the L. It's how my father says it. He grew up in Baltimore too, but I like it better from her. She takes my hand in hers and my breathing stops. "The Forge may not be perfect, I'm not saying it is, but you train people to defend themselves, right?"

I nod. It's true, that's a big part of what we do for those soft men we sneak out of the PS, if only so they can join us and fight for the Forge.

"I need that, Vale."

"It's not nice there, Ami, it's not safe for you." I don't know if I can keep her safe.

147

That innocent shrug again. "It's not safe anywhere, right? I might as well learn something besides paint colors and random words in Dena'ina."

She waits, patiently, letting her argument sit. Her eyes are a rich blue. I lean down to get a better look at them, only to find my focus straying to her lips, which fall open a fraction.

I want to kiss her. Before I can act on it, I do something else, anything else. I do the thing that might change this dynamic and get me out of the frustrating dance we're stuck in.

"Fine. Come with me."

A shadow of something—disappointment maybe— flashes over her face, before she does that thing where she sets her shoulders and lifts her chin.

Her hands fidget slightly now, pulling the zipper on her jacket and tugging on the two full halves of her ponytail, tightening it into place.

I take her hand and bring her with me, out of the alley and up toward the West High School complex.

We walk up Spenard Road, and when we turn onto Hillcrest I stop moving. I take the baseball cap off my head and hand it to her.

"Put this on, pull it down," I tell her and she nods, her eyes wide. She loops her ponytail through the back of the hat and pulls the rim low over her eyes. She takes a deep breath, a small smirk on her face.

"What?"

"It smells like you," she says.

"Sorry," I mutter.

She gives a slight shake of her head. "No, it's nice."

Okay. I scan her up and down one more time before we turn the bend and approach the guard station at the bridge.

"Do you have a weapon on you?" I ask. Ami nods.

"They'll find it. I can keep it in my backpack—they won't search me."

I say it more fiercely than I meant to. Her look is teasing. She caught that little outburst of overprotection. She pulls her jacket up, revealing a strip of smooth, tan skin and a sheath hooked onto the waistband. Ami carefully unhooks the knife and hands it to me, then bends down to pull a switchblade out of her boot.

A chuckle escapes me. "Deadly, aren't you?"

I tuck the knives into my bag and take a breath.

"I need you to give off your best don't-mess-with-me vibe, okay? Let me see it."

She tries to lift her chin and starts to giggle. She manages a straight face for a second before her shoulders shake. I throw up my hands in exasperation.

"That's not it, Pepper." There's something infectious about the sound of her laugh and I'm starting to chuckle, too. Without thinking I pull a tough guy face at her and she doubles over, laughing breathlessly.

"I'm Vale, get out of my way," she grunts, pulling the corners of her mouth down in a pout.

"I don't sound like that!" I complain, scandalized.

I pretend to tighten an imaginary ponytail. "I'm Ami, and I'm not afraid of anything."

"Hey." She shoves me and dissolves in another fit of giggles.

"Oh my God, Ami, we cannot go into the Forge like this," I say, wheezing.

"Of course we can," she gasps. "Hey, all you Forge men," she growls. "Don't mess with us."

I roll my eyes and lean against the light pole, waiting for her to pull herself together.

"Okay, okay." She straightens her spine.

"Are you ready?" I say, one more chuckle escaping me.

She puts her tough face on. "Of course. Come on, Vale, this is serious."

"Ami, don't," I warn, and I shove the laughter down before it overtakes me. We both shake ourselves out a little.

"Here we go," I say. "Follow my lead, okay?"

She raises her eyebrows at me. Who knows how this is going to go? Maybe I'll finally get some answers about what she's up to.

20

VALE

I USHER Ami past the guard stand and her attitude is perfect—cold, not forthcoming. Just gives her name and lets me say the rest. Her steady gaze is unnerving, so different from her giggles outside the complex.

She learns quickly, and she's already used to how things are up here. I think about her wandering the market. Now she walks beside me, spine straight, her hands shoved in the pockets of her coat. As I stare out of the corner of my eye I can't help but notice details of her profile.

Her freckles, still scattered over her cheeks all these years later. Her nose is straight, her chin pronounced. She moves with a smooth grace of practiced movement. Is she a dancer? She's broad in her shoulders, her upper back a dramatic V to her trim waist like maybe she rock climbs or wrestles. She wears it well, her pretty face and wavy brown hair on her athletic body.

Ami clears her throat. "Vale, you're staring."

I scoff a little. "Am not, you wish." *What am I, twelve years old now?*

There's a small smile on Ami's lips when her feet stop. In surprise I see we're at the wide front door. She looks at me expectantly and I try to hide my confusion. How did we get here so quickly?

"You know what," I start and falter, several things occurring to me at once. The minute we walk through those doors, my father will hear about it if he hasn't already from the guard in the booth out front.

Also, it's lunchtime and there will be men, lots of them, in the halls. I stray off the path, walking on the new June grass around the side of the building. Ami follows me without comment.

"Secret shortcut?" she asks under her breath.

"Something like that," I tell her. She crouches a little, like a sneaky spy. "Stop it," I say. I don't need her making me laugh right now. I come to a locked side door, steel, no handles, with narrow panes of glass covered over by plywood. I pull a key from my pocket.

"You live in a high school," Ami says.

"I live at the Forge," I tell her, pushing the key in and pulling as I turn to open the side door, which *is* in fact a secret shortcut.

"You know, I went to a high school like this," she says. "In Baltimore."

I roll my eyes as I pull the door open. "Not like this one, Ami."

We're in a back hall of what used to be the science wing. The labs have been converted into weapons storage. There are still a couple we use as labs, mostly for cooking up explosives and whatever else people are making—drugs, I don't know. Nothing good.

The original doors have been replaced by steel doors with padlocks. The lockers in the hall have been ripped out but not replaced, leaving a mess of plaster and plywood hanging off the walls. I hadn't thought about how it looks until I see Ami's wide eyes. Like a high school out of the apocalypse.

I take her quickly past the locker rooms where a few guys call out to us. She's got the hat pulled low over her eyes, and she stays right next to me. I couldn't ask for better cooperation.

We're quickly back to the offices and I unlock the door to my room, pulling her inside and locking the door with a sigh of relief.

Huh. I didn't think about where I was taking her. I remember thinking we would go and look for Zeph. Talk to them together, get some answers, and check her story. Instead she's in my room and I feel relief. At least she's not out in the Forge with all the men staring at her.

Ami's gazing at me. "Vale, you're nervous."

"No way," I mutter.

She smiles knowingly. "Your breathing. Your shoulders. I can tell."

I normally hate that PS stuff, monitoring everyone's emotional state at any given moment. But it makes sense for her to be on alert.

"I'm just worried for you. My father..." I'm not sure what to say about him.

"Isaiah Adamson," she murmurs.

"He's not a good man. I know that. He might have

been, a long time ago in Baltimore when my mom was still around."

Ami makes a noise in her throat at the mention of my mom and it doesn't help. I desperately push down the emotion before it can surface.

"The PS sent her to Iran. The negotiations in '26." There's more to the story that I don't want to discuss. I sit down heavily on the bed. Ami sits on the chair next to the desk, looking out the window at the water and the mountains. Her fingers trace over the empty desk.

I find myself drifting a little. It's a surreal experience to see her here in my space, sitting at my desk. I never thought I'd have a woman in here, especially one from the PS.

My father hates the PS for what happened to my mom, but he has something like respect for the leaders there. He figures, of course they emasculated men and grabbed power. But it makes sense to him that men would find a way out, find a way back to power.

Our legacy isn't a hatred of women, it's about becoming what we were meant to be.

"So, when can I talk to Zeph?" Ami shakes me out of my thoughts.

I nod, trying to figure out what to do, what to say.

"He's in basic training," I tell her.

"Training." She grins now, unexpectedly, widely, and leans towards me in the chair. "I like training," she says like she's admitting something embarrassing.

I snort. "What training have you done, Pepper?"

Ami gets haughty with me. "Citizen training is not

nothing, Your Majesty. And self-defense of course, and swim team," she adds.

Ah, swimming. That explains her strong build.

"Were you good?" I ask, suspecting the answer.

Ami avoids my gaze. "Probably," she says, looking up at the ceiling.

"What does that mean?"

She adds a shrug. "We don't compete in the traditional sense anymore."

Of course they don't. "I bet you were fast," I say.

She nods. "Do you swim?"

"A little. They have a pool over in the athletic building."

Ami's eyes shine. I like it.

"So can I join Zeph in basic training?" she asks.

I shiver. "No way. It's just men, Ami."

She nods. "What do women do? The ones who want to help the Forge?"

I'm not sure. There are a few partners scattered around the Forge, of course. My father has a woman who visits him, and some of the other lieutenants do as well. But I don't have a lot of exposure to any other women besides the ones I see when I'm undercover in the PS.

"The Forge is mostly men. There are women who are spies." I grimace a little. "Not too many. Spies mostly...or..."

"Or what?" she asks.

"Wives, girlfriends."

She nods, her face a mask suddenly. "Like the men in Maryland."

"No, it's not like that," I say fiercely. "It's what they want." Ami raises her pretty eyebrows at me.

"I want to do something," she says pointedly, making it clear she has no interest in hanging around as somebody's girlfriend.

I sigh. "We'll have to talk to my father about it."

"Any suggestions?" she asks.

"For what? Talking to him?"

"Yeah," she says, staring out the window now.

"He was trained by MAV back in the day. Be careful, he'll know all the tricks."

She turns back to me. "Tricks? You mean emotional regulation and control? It's not a trick, Vale."

I shrug. "It's a way to distract yourself from what you're really feeling and thinking, from your true natural reactions."

Her brow furrows. "Maybe humans aren't just meant to act naturally all the time. Maybe we're meant to evolve into compassionate people who work together and respect each other enough to not fly off the handle."

"The PS is not what you think," I tell her. "It hasn't been for a long time." I want to explain but there's a knock on my door. I jerk the door open and I'm glad Ami is sitting at my desk and not on the bed.

It's one of my father's guards and he laughs outright at the sight of Ami in my room, getting my hackles up immediately.

"Hey, pretty," he says to her first, his voice low and smooth. Ami smiles coyly from under my baseball hat.

"What do you want, Jones?" I demand.

"What do you think?" he shoots back. No sexy voice for me, I notice. "Your father wants to see you. Both of you," he adds.

Ami stands up and I don't like her obeying his orders without question. I stand still, keeping an eye on him. He moves to hold the door open for her, standing back with his eyes glued on her. Ami passes and his eyes travel rudely down.

"Nice," he whispers to me as I follow her.

"Shut up," I tell him flatly. "Keep your eyes to yourself." We hesitate outside the office. I don't want to follow him, but I'm not sure where my father is right now.

"Conference room, in the left wing," he says and starts to lead the way there.

"Leave it," I tell him, "I'll take her there myself."

He hesitates.

"I'll take her," I repeat, looking him directly in the eyes. This guy is a few years older than me, but he knows where I stand in the hierarchy.

"Sure you don't need some company?" he asks Ami.

She gazes back coolly. "We're good," she tells him, drawing closer to me.

His smile falls off his face. "Fine. You'd better get her there. I'm not taking the fall for you," he mutters and heads off in another direction.

I sigh. "Come on, Pepper. Let's get this over with."

OCTOBER 3, 2019

The world is watching as the US and North Korea prepare to meet. ("North Korea may have tested underwater-launched missile ahead of new nuclear talks with US"). I write these words not to the leaders in North Korea or the United States, but to the women in both of these countries.

Mothers know what it takes to bring a life into the world, to grow and raise a child. We must not let fellow humans be disposable. Every person's life is precious.

Join People Against Violence, formerly Mothers Against Violence. Already in the US we have changed liability and gun control laws. We have turned the right to own a gun into a privilege. We've dedicated millions of dollars and hours towards supporting and healing the victims of violence.

Women of North Korea, women of the world, and all who want peace, join our effort. Our contribution is essential, our legacy will be peace. Find out more at PAV.org.

Sincerely,
Mikayla Adamson
People Against Violence

21

AMITY

I REMEMBER what Vale told me about how to walk, how to act in the Forge, and I take a small centering breath, straightening to my full height.

It's like my calm face. Not whatever face I make when I'm naturally calm, but the mask they taught us in school. The waiting face, where you wait until you have your reactions and emotions under control. This is like that, but frownier. I'll have to come up with a name for this one. It could be my Tough Face. I smile a little and look around.

Unnervingly, men who are standing around the halls, in this complex that still feels so much like a high school, are staring straight back at me. Their eyes meet mine, and some of them have something dark in their gaze that sends a shiver through me.

I hurry to fix my face, wiping the smile away. Vale's body moves closer and when his hand brushes against mine he grabs hold of it, giving my palm a quick squeeze.

Now we're walking down the hall with our hands joined and he leans down to mutter into my ear.

"It's easier this way," he says, I guess about holding hands. "They'll know to leave you alone."

Know to leave me alone because I have his protection? Because I belong to him the way the women up here seem to belong to the men who claim them? I argue defiantly in my head about it, but outwardly I keep walking silently.

I'm tempted to look down, glimpse the sight of our hands folded together, but I keep my eyes trained on a spot in the distance, detached.

His hand is large and warm. A few times as we go down the stairs and walk through long hallways he readjusts the grip, one time lacing our fingers, later slipping his palm around mine to squeeze again when we have to pass through a crowded space outside the cafeteria.

I wish we were walking somewhere else. Walking on the trail at Herring Run, or browsing the shops in Hampden back in Baltimore.

We stop, finally, outside a room, and he drops my hand. A small placard, hanging from one side and covered in graffiti, says Teachers' Lounge.

I look over to Vale in question. He sighs and shakes his head slightly, knocking.

"Be as honest as you can," he murmurs. "He can tell..."

A voice calls from inside and we push into a wide room with a dingy carpet and blank cinderblock walls. If this was a teachers' lounge, it was a pretty wretched place.

There's a long table set up. Farther down the room, at the end of the table, sits Vale's father and two other men.

Isaiah Adamson stands and comes to greet us. He's like I remember, as tall as Vale, with the same dark brown skin like mahogany, with gray feathering his temples and cold brown eyes.

"I guess you two found each other," he says, and I can't tell who he is speaking to.

Vale nods. "Father, this is Ami." Vale's tone is tight, formal and something else. I wonder if he's afraid of his father.

"Sit down," his father says curtly. Vale and I pull chairs out and sit at the table and his father resumes his spot at the head.

There's silence. *I'm here, and this is what I'm doing,* I coach myself as I've coached my little brother, Ethan, so many times. *This is what is happening.* I glance around the room, locating myself in place to relieve the anxiety of the situation.

I catch Vale's dad studying me carefully, and I remember Vale said he was trained by MAV, that he knows all of the "tricks."

I want to ask about Zeph but I wait. The silence stretches. Vale cracks first.

"What? What do you need?" He's frustrated.

"Why don't you tell me what *you* want," Vale's dad says directly to me, "and we'll see what we can do."

"I want to talk to my friend Zeph, he's a new recruit," I say. The Peaceful Society wants me to do more than that. They want me to get involved with the organization, to learn more and report back to them.

I don't know if it's even possible, if women have any

role to play up here, but I have to try. "I want to work for the Forge, join the rebellion. There must be a way I can help."

Vale's father tilts his head.

"What do you know about the work we do here?" he asks finally.

"I know that you are trying to restore the Rights that were revoked in the PS. The right to assembly and, um, creative freedom," I list, thinking of Ren. "Movement and expression." I think of Zeph's father. "I know there are a lot of men who had to leave their families," I say, "and want to find a way back."

It's the most positive spin I can put on it. I'm not going to claim I want to fight on behalf of hurting and killing people. Vale said to be as honest as I can, and I think I've threaded the needle.

Isaiah Anderson eats it up, leaning forward, looking less distrustful.

"That's exactly right, Ami. The PS has placed their own priorities, their radical fringe beliefs, over family ties. What about the Rights of men in marriages? The right of men to father and raise children? Many of us were forced to leave our families and we've lost years and years of time, of memories and anniversaries, children's birthdays, just to accommodate how those women want to live," he says bitterly, his voice rising.

He leans back. "There *is* something you can do for the Forge."

Vale's head snaps over to his father. He had been watching me, I think.

"Both of you," his father adds, smiling. His smile is not exactly warm and comforting.

"I know who your mother is, and I don't trust you," he says to me, and I can't hold back a flinch. "No matter. You can't prove yourself to me with words. You can prove yourself with actions." He pauses, then says, "There's something we need, that the Brotherhood has."

At the confusion in my eyes Vale explains. "The Brotherhood is another militia on the west side of town."

"They have information about the government of Greater Maryland that we need," Isaiah tells us. "They tried to sell it to us but the price is too high. We have not been able to get it any other way."

Vale shifts uncomfortably in his seat, and I wonder, *What other ways did they try?*

Isaiah smiles again, but not with his eyes. "We've managed to get Vale an invitation to their solstice celebration this weekend. You will go as his girlfriend and the two of you will obtain the information we need. It's stored on a laptop in one of their offices."

Vale is stiff beside me. "What information?" he asks.

"That's classified," his father says immediately and chuckles.

He leans back in his chair, tilting it a little.

"This is a great opportunity to prove your loyalty, Ami."

"What about Zeph?" I ask.

He sighs, a bit exaggerated.

"Zeph is struggling in basic training," he says sorrowfully, and my heart thumps in my chest. "I'm not sure what his future holds, but your success in this little project will go a long way towards ensuring your friend's safety."

Vale sucks in a breath and I hear the warning and the threat behind the words. I push down my reaction, school my breathing carefully. I don't want Vale's father in my head.

"When is the party?" I ask quietly.

"The solstice is Saturday," Vale says. "The twenty-first."

I had lost track of time, but that makes sense given how sunny it is here even when I lie down to go to sleep at night.

His dad stands and Vale pushes his chair back. He grabs my hand, defiantly, and we walk to the door together.

"We'll follow up," his father says, looking at Vale. Vale nods and opens the door, pulling me through.

Once we're out in the hall with the door closed, he breathes deeply a couple of times and shakes his head.

"We get to work together," I say.

"Something is up," Vale answers me quietly. "I'll find out more."

"Stealing a laptop." I shrug. "How hard can it be?"

Vale's eyes widen. "They'll be watching me. The Brotherhood and the Forge are not on good terms, especially lately. Maybe this is why."

"Then why would they let you come to their solstice party?" I ask.

Vale shakes his head. "Can't be a good reason, Ami, I'll be honest."

"It'll be okay," I say reflexively, although there's no way I can know that.

Vale stares off in the distance. I realize we've been .

walking down the hall into a new part of the school when I pass the glass panes of a weight room filled with squat racks and punching bags. There's a slight smell of chlorine in the air that has me sniffing curiously.

Vale notices. Of course he does.

"Ami," he says. "Do you want to go swimming?"

22

AMITY

"VALE," I mutter, my cheeks heating up, "I don't have anything to swim in."

"We have extra. I'm sure there's some women's suits. Let's at least check," he says.

"You don't have to do that," I protest.

Vale nods, looking resigned. "You think I'm going to be better than you, don't you? I understand."

I shove him. "Are you kidding? I swam every day for five years." I shake my head at him. "Really, Vale, I could be your swimming teacher."

There's a light of something in his eyes. "You think you can beat me, Pepper?"

"I know I can," I say, raising my eyebrows.

"Okay, come on, big talker." He takes my hand and half drags me to a door labeled "Pool Supplies." The smell of chlorine is even stronger here and the small room is filled with brushes, nets, and chemicals in tubs. There's a washer and dryer in the corner, and Vale rifles through a bin next to the dryer. He pulls out shorts and a one-piece women's swimsuit and throws it over.

"There. No excuses, big swimmer."

"Afraid you'll lose to a girl from the PS?" I bait him and step behind a line of shelves piled high with filters and test kits. I strip down and pull the suit on as I hear the rustle of his clothing. Trying not to think too hard about that, I grab a towel from a stack behind me and wrap it around my waist.

Gathering up my clothes, I call, "You good?"

Vale makes an affirmative sort of grunt and I peek around the shelves. His back is to me. He's got swim trucks on so I step out shyly. I'm glad the swimsuit I'm wearing is more of an athletic cut.

My eyes trace the ripple of muscle from his wide shoulders down to his waist. There's something marring his skin—darker lines. Apparently, Vale's survived quite a few cuts and injuries. The scars look old. He must have gotten hurt a lot when he was younger. My heart aches and I must make a little noise because he whips around, his eyes wary.

I want to say something, but I'm distracted by the intensity of his gaze, the slight upward curve of his lips. I see his eyes rest on the rounded cut of my shoulders.

"What?" I ask belligerently. The women up here may be weaker than the men, but that's not the case in the PS. I'm strong, and tall like my mom. "Getting cold feet now, Your Highness?"

He shakes his head, leading the way over to a side door that opens directly into the pool area. There are a bunch of men doing laps. I missed this, the soft splashing, the crawl of swimmers through the water. Something inside me lights up.

"Come on," Vale says and jumps in with a splash. He treads water. "Come on, Pepper, the water's fine," he calls, dunking again and shaking the water off.

I stare at him in the pool while I stretch; the water is dripping off him. I don't think he knows how...appealing he looks.

Vale laughs, sending a spray of water toward me, and kicks off the wall, swimming easily down the lap lane. I finish stretching and step in the pool, letting the cold water envelop me, shivering a little. They keep this pool much cooler than the one I use in Baltimore. I let the cold invigorate me and kick off the wall, warming up.

Vale didn't lie. He's a competent swimmer, smooth and practiced. I duck into the lane next to him, and we swim a couple of easy laps, warming up before he kicks into high gear. I don't catch him before he gets to the end. He pauses at the wall, grinning back at me.

"Guess I won."

"That wasn't winning," I say, exasperated. "You sped up. You had a head start!"

"*Was* it a head start?" he asks quizzically, teasing me. "Or did you just start late?"

"Okay, hotshot," I say, clinging to the wall and counting down. "Five, four, three, two, one..."

This time we both shoot out at the same time, and I let my legs kick hard. I have a faint impression of Vale beside me, but he's slightly behind me as I finish, coming up in triumph.

He sputters as he finishes after me. "I'm still warming up," he complains, grinning.

"Sure you are."

His arms, holding him up on the shelf, have the same faint scar lines as his back. There's a big one tracing down his left forearm.

"Vale, what happened to you?" I ask quietly.

He doesn't answer, glancing away, out to the rest of the pool, before turning back to face me. "Why'd you cut your hair?" he asks without answering my question.

This time I look away. I can't talk to him about that. He nods grimly. We both have secrets.

"Let's do some laps," he says, changing the subject.

I nod. "Yeah."

He starts again, swimming at a slower tempo this time, and I begin my routine, starting with the crawl before moving to the backstroke. I see him now and then and he keeps going, steady, not taking breaks.

He's right. He is a swimmer. He's lasting longer than I thought he would, keeping up a steady pace. Beside him I find myself pushing harder, showing off a little. When he finally stops I glance up at the clock and it's been half an hour of steady swimming. We're both breathing hard and deep, recovering.

His smile is respectful. "Thanks, Ami. I feel better."

"That was great," I agree. "I haven't swum since I got up here. I really appreciate it."

"Just find me. We can come here anytime," he assures me, pushing up and out of the water. I blink a little at his triceps.

"Um, yeah." I push out myself. "I should, uh, probably get back."

Vale nods. "I'll walk you out."

"You don't have to do that," I tell him, a little formally. He shrugs.

"Yeah, I do."

We duck back through the side door and I get dressed again behind the shelving, rubbing as much water off with a towel as I can before pulling my clothes on. My hair is dripping and I rub it with the same towel, wringing the water out.

Luckily it's not too cold out today. I'll take a shower when I get back.

"What should I do with this?" I ask, coming out. Vale is dressed. He throws his suit in the open washing machine with his towel.

"In here is fine."

"Okay." I follow him out, zipping up my jacket. There's a side door out of the athletic complex onto the grounds. We follow a pathway that has us circling around, back toward the front.

The whole complex is shut off with fencing and roads, and all the entrances are guarded. There are old sports fields back here, but instead of empty grass with paint marking the fields, they're filled with trucks.

Rows and rows of eighteen-wheelers are lined up on what looks like the former football field. On the basketball and tennis courts there are dozens of school buses. I stop short, caught off guard by all the vehicles.

I peer down the aisle between them, and the rows go on and on until the fence of the complex, maybe half a mile away. I glance toward Vale, who is scanning the scene also. His face reflects the surprise I feel.

"That's a lot of trucks," I say.

"Yeah." Vale doesn't add anything, just leads me past. I spot men moving through the vehicles, looking them up and down, bending down to check underneath, like they're doing an inspection.

"What does the Forge do with...?" I start to ask but Vale cuts me off in a low voice.

"Don't ask. I shouldn't have brought you back here. Come on." He leads the way between two buildings to scrubby grass in the front and the guard booth on the bridge where we came in.

"Is the Forge shipping something? Or moving somewhere?" I mutter, my mind racing to explain the vehicles. Vale shakes his head.

"It's classified," he tells me with finality, sounding a bit like Isaiah. But he still looks perplexed. "Let's just do this thing for my father and I'll try to figure out what's going on with the trucks."

"They're not always here?" I ask quickly, noting his confusion.

"No. Well, I've been away. I don't know everything that's happening."

I'm not sure I believe that. I shiver, the air is cool on my wet hair.

"Here." I hand him back his baseball hat. "Sorry it's a little wet."

"Keep it," he says. "What about Saturday, where should we meet? Can I come to you, and we can get organized before we go?"

I wonder what getting organized looks like. I've tried to hide where I'm living, and I'm pretty sure Vale didn't follow me home any of the days we met up at the market.

I consider for a second and he waits, patient, for me to decide. It's one of those things that reminds me so much of the Peaceful Society, of home. I know Vale was raised up here but he's so...patient. It's not the vibe I get walking the streets of Anchorage. He quietly pulls my knives out and hands them back to me.

"Yeah, you can come over," I agree. I put the knife away and shove the switchblade into my pocket as I give him the address. Vale pulls a phone out of his pocket.

"Should I get your number?" he asks.

"No." I shake my head, smiling a little. "I'll see you Saturday."

MARCH 31, 2020

Governor Hogan is taking dramatic steps to save lives that are threatened by the novel coronavirus ("Gov. Hogan issues stay-at-home order for Maryland to stop spread of the coronavirus"). We are all being asked to make sacrifices for the public good.

The worldwide group People Against Violence supports all public health measures to slow or stop the spread of the virus. We're delighted to hear of truces and ceasefires breaking out around the globe in an effort to avoid infection.

Just as the fear of disease and death can inspire us to take action to protect people, fear of injury and death from violence and war should inspire the same action. Along with sending masks and medical supplies abroad to save lives, we must *stop* sending weapons that take lives. People Against Violence is calling for Congress to pass the Halt Weapons Sales Act of 2020.

Every bomb not sold is a home or building left standing, another family intact. Every child saved from military violence is a child who will grow up strong and resilient in a loving world. Support the Halt Weapons Sales bill: call your representatives today.

Sincerely,
Mikayla Adamson
People Against Violence

23

VALE

FOR SOME REASON it feels different, quieter, once Ami is out of sight, walking back down Spenard. I stand for a few more minutes, gazing out, letting the sun warm me through my clothes. I feel a strange tingle, almost a burning in my throat, and find myself wishing she had stayed a little longer. It feels worse here without Ami.

I shake myself and head inside, my mind flicking back and forth from the image of Ami sitting at my room, at my desk, facing the window, to the sight of her swimming in the pool.

The throat feeling intensifies, and I wonder if I'm coming down with something. I head to the cafeteria and grab a big glass of water, chugging it down. The sounds of clinking silverware, clattering plates, and the low voices of the Forge are familiar. After I drink the water I feel better.

A lot of times the cafeteria annoys me. All the people, all the commotion. I'd rather eat alone in my room. But the thought of taking a plate up to my empty room, eating alone at the desk where Ami was sitting...shoot, my throat is burning again. I blink rapidly as my eyes itch. I'll take something for allergies before bed.

I decide to stay down here, not ready to face the silence of my room with only thoughts of Ami for company.

I scan for her friend Zeph, and my feet take me over to him once I have a full plate of food in my hands. Zeph looks tired, beaten down, as all the new recruits do. The mental and physical training my father has designed for them is no joke.

I went through it, in addition to all the extra training sessions he required me to do. I sit across from Zeph and he glances up, wary.

"Ami just left," I say. I don't know why, I'm not trying to tease him or make him feel bad. It's just what I'm thinking about.

Zeph's head swings around as if he might still catch a glimpse of her. "Here at the Forge?" His voice hardens. "Why was she here?" He's suspicious. "And why didn't I get to see her?"

"We're still not sure what she's up to."

"I'm sure," he argues. "She followed me here. I want to see her," he says, louder.

"Calm down. I'm filling you in. I didn't have to come over here. I'm trying to understand. It seems like she had everything back there, with her mom serving in the military, and the swimming and HighClear and everything."

His face clouds.

"What?" I ask a little more forcefully than I mean to. "Is there something you're not telling me?"

"No, you're right." He shakes his head. "Ami had a good life in the Society—the PS—" he corrects himself. "But she wasn't happy. Not lately." He stares off in the distance.

"When did you meet her?" I ask

"We moved onto the block after the Integration," he explains.

Ah. He must have come after I left.

"I think a lot of people moved away, but when Ami and I met it was like, this is great. We went everywhere together."

I'm hit with an unexpected wish to have been there too, having adventures with them. Or to have been the new kid, taken under Ami's wing.

"What do you mean everywhere?" I try to remember Baltimore. My mom took me to parks and I played in our alley or at a friend's house.

"All over the city. There were no cars or anything," he explains.

The Peaceful Society banned cars while they were ramping up public transit, before they allowed e-cars.

"And there were the security stations." He lowers his voice, looking apologetic.

I know the men here hate them, but I don't care. I want to hear more about Ami. "Where would you go?"

"Everywhere. Every alley, every corner store. Ami had a bunch of places she liked to visit."

"Like where?" I can't help asking.

"The Y or the pool, the record shop, a chocolate shop, the old brewery."

He laughs as my face twists. "They weren't selling beer, but they had pinball machines in the back. You know, the library. She liked to be out all day. We'd take the bus, just to see where it went." He's grinning.

I try to imagine it. If we'd stayed in Baltimore, it could have been me as a young teenager, wandering free. Even after we escaped the PS and came up here, I was never free to explore like that. We had to stay in the compound. It was years of learning to defend myself before my father would trust me out in Anchorage without a guard babysitting me.

"What changed?" I ask, remembering he said Ami didn't seem that happy lately.

"She just..." He stops to think. "It's a lot of pressure on the girls, you know, the ones going up for Clearance. To be smart, and strong, and master all the regulation stuff. Yeah," he muses. "The more advanced she got with her self-control, the more she seemed shut down a lot of the time. She'd do homework with me, or take a walk on the weekend. But she changed a lot.

"I get it," he goes on. "She had to do everything, be everything, and do it all well. She didn't allow herself to explore or try new things, even though that was what she loved, you know, before."

We lapse into silence, eating while the murmurs rise and fall around us. Finally I glance up and Zeph is staring at me.

"Okay, I told you about her," he says a little coldly. "Now when do I get to see her?"

I consider the possibilities, but there's no way I'm letting him get involved with the mission at the Brotherhood on the solstice this weekend. It'll be hard enough keeping Ami safe there; I don't need an untrained recruit on top of it.

"At least tell me where she's staying and I can say hi to her," he complains.

My eyes flick to my phone where I wrote down her address. He's watching me closely. I shake my head no. I'll have to check with my dad before I give this guy her info and send him out into Anchorage, maybe go with him to supervise. I know the drill with new recruits. They're stuck in the compound until they're fully trained and trustworthy.

"I'm sorry I can't share that," I tell him. His eyes dart to my phone, but I pick it up and shove it in my pocket. He's stuck. Unless he wants to sneak out and roam Anchorage looking for a needle in a haystack, he'll have to wait until I get the all clear.

"I'll ask my father about it, let you know what he says," I assure Zeph.

He doesn't seem upset, just thoughtful. "And what do you think he'll say?"

I shrug, pushing my chair back. "Probably no. But I'll check with him anyway."

I stride away from the table, trying to leave behind all thoughts of Ami and focus on what I need to do next. But even as I step out into the quiet hallway, I suddenly remember what she smells like.

I need to get myself back in the zone. I waffle between going straight to my dad or to my room. I'll head back to my room and shower first.

My room is no better. Not with the memories of Ami, perched on the chair, looking out the window at the mountains. Even the smell of chlorine clinging to me reminds me of her. I scrub, trying to leave the scent and the memories behind, focus myself and my breathing.

I can't be distracted while I'm talking to my father, I need to be perfectly focused. I breathe deeply, taking a minute to find my center before I head out.

24

AMITY

I CAN'T STOP SMILING, and I decide it's because I got to swim after missing so many days. It's not so bad up here, I think happily as I look far into the distance at the still white-capped mountains.

When I pull open the door to the house I'm hit by the strong smell of paint. The windows are wide open but the fumes are still strong inside. Ren is up on a ladder, a few splatters of paint on their overalls, vigorously rolling lime green paint onto the living room walls. The paintings and posters have been taken down and they're piled everywhere.

"Hi, Ren," I say faintly, trying not to breathe too deeply. Ren should probably be wearing a mask or something but instead they seem to be in the middle of shouting a violent story into the next room.

"Basically, everyone in the Midwest gets killed by robots, but not by killer robots, more like locked in their houses and not allowed to leave."

I blink. I'm pretty sure that's not what happened in the Midwest.

"I don't see what killer robots have to say about human systems of justice and imprisonment," an unfamiliar male voice shouts back from the kitchen.

I haven't moved. I'm watching the green paint spread on the wall as Ren wrestles with the roller, continuing the discussion.

"The robots are meant to represent our own inability to effect positive change and free will in our own lives. And they're scary robots, which makes it exciting!"

A man walks through the door. "Come on, that's a cheap trick. You need to show humans choosing their own destiny, to show the imagined limitations the proto-communist system places around the individual."

I'm guessing this is Eli. He turns from the green paint to me.

"You must be Ami. I'm Eli," he says.

"Hi," I say.

Ren scoffs. "You'd make a terrible storyteller."

Rather than talk to me more, Eli whirls on Ren.

"Revolution is all about storytelling. It's an integral part of what we do. You can't convince people to act until they believe a story that shows them why it's necessary."

"And how's that going?" Ren asks sardonically, climbing down to dip the roller.

Eli looks uncomfortable. "We're still beta testing. Anyway, our story is better than a bunch of human-starving robots. Sounds boring."

"Don't you worry about that," Ren says a little smugly. "Wait till you read it and then tell me it's boring."

They must be talking about a story Ren's writing. I remember they told me they write stories with, and I quote, "lots of violence."

"Eli," a voice comes from the kitchen. "Let them work. Can you help me with the vegetables?"

I follow Eli into the kitchen, coughing a little from the fumes. The windows are open in here too. With the fan blowing, it's easier to breathe.

Moira—Ren's friend? Girlfriend?—is at the kitchen counter, but she's not chopping the pile of little carrots in front of her. She's got a sketchbook open and she's staring at the page.

"Here I am," Eli grumbles as Moira doesn't look up. "Are we working or not?"

"Oh, yeah." Moira jumps a little. "Sorry, trying to finish this design for the mural." She shoves the sketchbook aside and assigns Eli asparagus and asks if I can work on shelling peas. I take the peas and a second bowl over to the table and figure out how to pry them open. Out pop the peas, one, two, three, four. It's surprisingly satisfying.

"I just think they could write something that would help the people see the need to band together and create a new system of shared power," Eli grumbles to Moira. From Moira's face, this tension between Eli and Ren is not new. "They're selling out to fulfill the bloodlust of the masses without a sense of higher purpose."

"*And* their writing keeps food on this table," Moira points out. "Heaven knows, more than my art or Qilan's translations. And the revolution's not a big money maker," she adds gently.

"Our future together is more important than our

comfort now." Eli waves a stick of asparagus around in the air. "And where are you coming from?" he asks, turning to me.

Moira sighs.

"I was at the Forge. I have a friend there." I wonder to myself who I'm talking about. Zeph? Vale? "And yeah," I add as Eli opens his mouth, presumably to tell me how bad and dangerous the Forge is, "I know how bad and dangerous they are."

Eli settles a little, deflated. Now he stares at me curiously, cocking his head. "This is your first time out of the PS, right?"

"Yeah," I agree.

"Eli," Moira mutters. "Asparagus."

He turns back to washing and breaking the ends off the asparagus but continues, "I've never been there."

"And be glad you haven't," Ren shouts from the other room.

Eli shakes his head. "I don't agree with everything they've done, but at least they've set up a system with an eye to universal."

"Because they deport everyone who disagrees with them!" Ren pipes up again.

"Is forcible relocation the only way to establish a society without conflict?" Eli muses. "Or do you need to plan for some amount of conflict inherent in our imperfect biology, and build a system able to withstand the naturally occurring aggressive impulses?"

"Now you sound like Vale," I tell him. "With that biology stuff."

Eli thinks about that.

"Less philosophizing, more chopping," Moira directs again.

"Listen to my girlfriend," Ren shouts from the other room. A little harried now, Eli continues breaking the ends off the asparagus while Moira dumps a bag of dried pasta into bubbling water.

"Putting the pasta in," she calls to Ren.

"Okay, I'll be there in a minute," Ren says back. They're so domestic, it's sweet.

"Is Qilan here? Should I call her?" I ask.

"No, she's down at the Dena'ina library, she won't be back until later. Just us tonight."

I pry open the last few pods, waiting to see if Eli's got more to say about the Peaceful Society or the Forge, but he's quiet now, staring thoughtfully at the asparagus as he finishes up and then works on grating cheese.

We end up eating out on the front porch, which has a few pieces of dumpy furniture shoved into the corners, since the table was covered with pictures and knickknacks from the living room.

The meal, bowls of pasta with vegetables and sauce and cheese, is delicious. It's sweet to hear Moira quietly thanking Ren for painting and Eli chiming in.

"Oh, you know, I need something to do with my hands when I'm not writing. How's the mural shaping up?" Ren asks.

It turns out Moira's working on the design for a mural she's going to paint at the market. "They're not paying me exactly." She's embarrassed. "But they'll buy the paint for it."

"It's a good gig," Ren says. "Moira was chosen from a dozen painters to do it."

I smile at the pride in Ren's voice.

"I can't wait to see it," I tell them.

"Oh, you'll probably get to help," Eli chuckles. "When Moira's working on a big project we all end up covered in paint."

Moira is affronted. "You like helping! You say manual labor is the religion of the righteous worker."

They both laugh. "That's the only reason I help," Ren jokes.

"Not true." Moira digs her elbow into Ren's side.

"Okay, that and the paint fumes," Ren says, taking a deep breath.

I cringe. "You should wear a mask in there."

"Thank you!" Moira says to me loudly and Ren looks a little guilty.

We sit out after dinner while the sun is still bright, even as it gradually sinks in the sky. The nights don't get fully dark here, just sort of twilight-y, so it's still pretty light out when I start to yawn.

I'm thinking of heading inside when I feel the others fall quiet rapidly and stiffen. There's someone approaching, peeling off from the street and coming up the walk, wearing dark camo like the men at the Forge with a hat pulled low over his eyes.

I tense. Glancing around, the man pulls the hat off and glances up at the porch, directly at me. He's got red hair and pale skin with freckles, even more freckles than I do. It's Zeph.

25

AMITY

"OH MY GOODNESS," I gasp and spring up, rushing down the stairs. I throw my arms around Zeph and we hug. He squeezes me tight and I try not to choke up. I was so worried about him.

I pull back to look at him. He has dark rings under his eyes, and he's paler than I remember from Baltimore, but he looks okay otherwise. A little thin. Tired. I probably look the same way.

"Amity," he mutters with a glance up at the porch to where everyone is sitting, watching with interest. "What are you doing up here?"

I glance back and everyone looks down, Ren clearing their throat and asking Moira a question about the mural she's painting.

"Let's, um, walk around the block," I say, taking Zeph's hand and dragging him.

"We'll be right back," I call to the others.

"Everything okay?" Eli's standing now, watching me.

"It's my friend Zeph, from Baltimore. It's okay," I say, then glance around, not wanting all the neighbors to hear my business.

Zeph looks wary and starts walking. I hurry to catch up.

"I can't believe this," he says to me. "I can't believe you came up here, Amity."

"Ami," I correct him. He looks like he's suppressing a smile. "Ami? That's what Vale was calling you. Trying out something new?"

I shrug. "Trying to stay under the radar a little bit. My mom and my family... you know."

"Yeah," he agrees, and I feel his eyes sweep me as I am searching for signs he's okay.

"I can't believe you refused your oath," he says quietly.

I guess he can't believe any of this. It's starting to grate a little. This is when I need to lie. Maybe I can skirt the truth a little bit.

"I can't believe it either. But also, Zeph, there's so much I didn't know about the world. We never left Maryland after the Integration, you know."

"Yeah." He nods. "It's pretty different up here."

"Everything is different. Canada is...crazy."

"Did you drive through the Midwest?" he asks.

I shake my head no.

"That part was pretty nice, actually," he says. "Everyone's on UBI. And all the citizens are treated... equally."

When I think about how men are treated back in the PS, I cringe. I was always told there were good reasons for it. Historically, men committed the most murders and acts of violence, and men had biological reasons to be more aggressive and less in control of their emotional state.

I expect Zeph to say how much better it is up here, but when I turn to him there's worry creasing his brow.

"Maybe you should head there. To the Midwest," he says.

That's not what I was expecting him to say.

"Why?"

"It's not safe for you here. They don't treat women well at all. The Forge, the other group, the Brotherhood. Women are second-class citizens. And you don't have anyone looking out for you."

He doesn't say "any man" but I know what he means.

"I'm learning to look out for myself," I argue. "And I have my roommates."

Zeph rolls his eyes.

"Hey, they're great," I say, giving him a little shove.

"I'm sure they are, Ami," he says my new name a little carefully. "But are you training? Learning to shoot?"

"That's what I want to learn from the Forge," I burst out.

Zeph huffs. "They'll never let you train with the men."

"You sound like Vale," I tell him.

"Look, you can't trust that Vale guy. He's been up here with his dad, who is vicious, working for him all these years."

"Says the guy who joined their little club," I argue.

Zeph shakes his head. "I'm telling you. Stay away from the Forge."

"How did you find me?" I ask, changing the subject.

"Vale's phone," Zeph says a little guiltily. "He doesn't have very strong security on it."

"Do they know you can do that?" I ask with a grin. Zeph always could figure out a way to get around cyber defenses and firewalls.

"I'm sure they'll figure it out eventually," he returns my grin.

"What if we train together, the two of us?" I suggest.

"I had to sneak out for this. I don't think I'll be able to do it again. Besides, I might not even be up here that long."

I'm puzzled.

"I think we're moving down to West Virginia," he says.

"West Virginia? That's right next to Greater Maryland."

"They say they're going to work something out with the PS. Bring the two groups back together."

"Work something out?" My voice rises. "The Forge is going to work something out with the PS? No way." I can't believe it.

He shrugs.

"They're lying about that," I say, not willing to mince words at this point, especially if I might not get to see him again. "They're probably planning an attack. Do you think you could attack your own home?" I say a little accusingly.

"That's not the plan," he says defensively. "We're going to negotiate."

We turn the last corner. Ren's house is down the street on the right.

We've walked around the block so many times over the years, me and Zeph, but it's never felt like this. I don't know how many more chances we'll get.

"How did this happen to us?" I say, before I can stop it.

Zeph laughs darkly.

"Do you miss Miro?" I wonder.

Zeph doesn't answer yes or no. "We broke up anyway."

"Oh, I didn't know, I'm sorry."

"He didn't agree with…this." He looks up, and around, at the houses, at Anchorage, at the mountains in the distance. And then at me.

"I'm still not sure what I think," I say, and it's the truth. "But I know I don't trust the Forge," I tell him fiercely.

"Do you trust the PS?" he asks.

I shake my head no. It's partially true, but I'm still taking orders when they come through the secure messaging app.

"Vale asks about you a lot," Zeph says a little slyly.

"What does he ask about?" I demand.

"Today he was asking about when you were a kid, what you were like."

"Did he tell you I knew him back then?"

"Yeah. Sounds like we just missed each other," Zeph says.

"But you don't trust him," I repeat from earlier.

Zeph is quiet, thinking. "I trust him more than his father. He seems to care about you, be worried for you. Maybe talk to him about the Midwest thing, Amity. Promise me you'll consider it."

"It's Ami now," I say. "I'll think about it."

We're back to the house and Zeph looks around, pulling his hat lower over his face. "I probably need to get back."

"Are you sure you don't want to come in for tea or something?" I ask a little hesitantly.

"No, I don't want them to miss me. New recruit and all," he says.

I nod. "Yeah, okay. Be careful."

"I'll be careful," he assures me. "Don't worry about me."

I try to digest everything he said as I walk up the steps. The couches are empty now. Everyone's gone inside and the sky is finally turning an orangey-pink as it gets later. I go straight to my room and pull the shade down to try to get some sleep.

WASHINGTON POST *LETTERS TO THE EDITOR*

JANUARY 24, 2021

I'm glad to see coverage in the *Washington Post* of the crime reduction plan put out by our new mayor ("Baltimore mayor proposes stripping police of weapons"). I'm asking the *Post* to consider being more specific and accurate in their descriptions and headlines in the future.

Our new mayor, Angela Coleman of the People Against Violence party, has not suggested that police in Baltimore carry no weapons. As part of her new plan, City Without Guns, she is proposing that police carry *non-lethal* weapons. This plan will continue the sharp drop in shootings and murders that has already taken place in Baltimore.

The more that people in our city, including police, feel they are in danger, the greater the chance they will carry a gun for protection and be tempted to use it. We must bit by bit, step by step, make it *feel* safer, in addition to making it *be* safer.

The police officers will still carry weapons, including Tasers and batons, and still have the option to call for backup with lethal weapons. However, people on the streets of the city will take comfort in knowing the same rules apply to everyone. No one is allowed to carry a gun. No one is allowed to put others at risk.

Post readers could push for the same in their own city. If you want to know what it feels like to walk around in a City Without Guns, come to Baltimore. It could be like that in your city as well. PAV candidates are running for DC Council and Mayor.

Sincerely,
Mikayla Adamson
Baltimore, Maryland
People Against Violence

26

VALE

THIS JOB my father has given us is crazy. Just to go to a party at the Brotherhood is dangerous enough. If they want to start something with me, we'll be swamped with Brothers. In my mind I see me and Ami, surrounded by dozens of Brotherhood men.

Going there could be a trap, and my father wants me to steal from them. The stuff he said in front of Ami was vague and not helpful, so I'm going to get the answers now.

Where exactly is this laptop in their compound? Finding and stealing are two different tasks, so unless my father has a location for us, I'm not going to be searching their compound top to bottom. The Brotherhood will keep an eagle eye on me. And Ami? She's gorgeous, and confident. She's bound to attract attention.

A wiggle of discomfort nags at me. If what we're doing up here, in Anchorage, is the right thing, why do the women look so different from Ami? So scared all the time? Memories of my mom, faded a little, hit me. My mom was intelligent, tall and strong, a military veteran. My father used to say she was the best of the best. I never saw her shrink back or cower.

My whole life is spent around men now. It seems natural up here for men to be in charge—we're the ones always working and planning.

I'm not sure what women do anyway, raise children, watch the babies. They help with the cooking. They're not out there risking their necks or training with the men. But maybe they would if they had the chance? I shake my head. I'm not sure what to think.

Standing, I reach to grab my hat from the hook but it's not there. Oh yeah, I gave my hat to Ami.

I'm thinking about her again. I stare out the window into the wide parking lot in front of the Forge, but I'm seeing Ami in her swimsuit, thinking about the cut of her arms through the water. I take a deep breath. She could still be a PS spy. I need to stay cool, stay detached.

It's dangerous, how she distracts me.

I text my father and he answers to come to his room. I head down the stairs. My father's room is all the way in the basement, in the old storage rooms. It's a smart place for a leader. Not out on top, not the fanciest, but down here, hidden, hard to find. The corridor is dark with lights that need to be replaced, but he likes it that way. I knock on his door, which has Employees Only stenciled on the front.

It jerks open and he stands in the doorway. I scan the room quickly. He's alone.

He sees me do it. My father doesn't miss anything.

"Just us," he says. "I need to tell you something."

Interested, I look up. It's not always clear when he wants me to answer him, and a long time ago I learned to err on the side of silence.

The room has low ceilings, not much higher than the tops of our heads. There's a small kitchen, a couch, and rooms behind, a bedroom and bathroom.

"Vale," he says, taking a seat at the table. I mimic him. Scattered across the surface are papers I recognize, old newspaper clippings with letters from Mikayla Adamson. My mom was a great writer. She used to write to the *Baltimore Sun* on behalf of MAV all the time.

"I need to tell you something."

He already said that. I wonder where this is going. Is it about Ami?

"It's about your mother." I flinch. My mom died many years ago at Natanz, at the nuclear site there. The PS sacrificed her with no compassion; Ami's grandmother Selene Bloome sent her there knowing how dangerous it was. She never returned from that last, deadly mission.

"Vale. There is new information we've heard. Rumors that your mother might be alive."

"What? What do you mean?" I ask him. Eight years she's been gone. They didn't care that she had a ten-year-old kid. Just ripped her away from her family and sent her to her death.

"It's information from Western Maryland, from the camps there."

The camps outside of Frederick? I shudder. It's where the PS keeps men who have been deemed a threat. Too dangerous to put on the depo trains. They say they emptied the jails when the PS was formed, but really they just shipped men off to camps.

"She's being held there?" I ask.

"We don't know. Someone made contact with a prisoner at one of the camps. The prisoner said she's there. They were sure it was her." He ducks his head and I see he's feeling emotional. I'm still in shock.

"How could she be alive this long and we didn't know?"

"She's going by another name is what they said: 'Kayla Davis.'"

"Davis?" I ask.

"It was her name before we married. Her maiden name."

"Is she a prisoner or is she…" I trail off.

"One of them?" My father grimaces. "We think she's a prisoner."

I realize if she's not a prisoner, if she's been working for the PS this whole time, it means she left me willingly. Left my father with a kid to take care of and never looked back.

A sudden thought occurs to me. "Do you think she left because I was a boy?"

My father's face is a mask, but I can see pain behind it. He shakes his head slowly.

"No, Vale. She loved you so much. It didn't matter to her that you weren't a girl."

My eyes sting. I believe him. His eyes shine a little bit, and I wonder if he will cry.

"It wasn't perfect," he mutters, "but we were a family together. She believed in us, believed in our future."

"But she also believed in MAV? Mothers Against Violence?"

"Of course," he snaps. "We all did. A new world. A legacy of peace," he says bitterly. "The revoking of Rights, it was only supposed to be temporary. Once everyone understood they lived in a world without danger, a world of perfect peace or whatever, we'd all get our Rights back. But it didn't happen. Privilege." He says the word bitterly. "It's just a way to keep men down."

His breathing is more ragged now.

"What can we do?" I try to focus him.

His face settles into grim determination. He jerks open a drawer in front of him and pulls out a cylinder.

We both stare at it. In training, we practice with these. It contains a needle, a quick shot to the neck with a drug that knocks you out immediately. We train to avoid them. They are one of the PS's main weapons for fighting and controlling men. This one looks different.

"Is that real?" I ask.

"Yes, this is PS made and approved," he says, turning it over, and I see a lot of tiny writing on the other side. He jerks the cap off, holds it against the table. "Press and it should happen in under ten seconds." Knocking the person unconscious.

"Who's it for?" I ask.

"It's for you. Take it. If the girl turns on you, use it on her."

"And leave her with the Brotherhood?" I ask angrily. I have no intention of doing that.

"Watch her, Vale. If she helps, if she proves trustworthy, then bring her back. Otherwise…"

Otherwise leave her. I shudder. I'm not doing that. I'll carry her out over my shoulder if I have to.

"The laptop is in their security station on the roof," he tells me.

On the roof? "How are we going to get onto the roof?" I ask. More importantly, how am I going to get down off the roof and out of their compound—with a laptop and Ami?

"Find a way in, find a way out," my father snaps. "We need this done before we begin the move."

"It's really happening?"

"Yes. We've got hundreds of trucks and buses to load up before we go. The information on that laptop is what we need to get into the camps around Frederick, find out for sure about your mother."

He doesn't seem sad anymore, only deadly and determined. His hand shakes slightly and he grips the table, pushing the injection device over to me. "Get me that laptop."

"What's on it? And what are you going to do about Mom?" I ask him.

He regards me coolly now, not answering right away. I'm definitely the only one who's allowed to talk to him like this.

"Father, can you just explain the whole thing?" I say in frustration, sensing he's not telling me everything.

"I'm not putting all my eggs in one basket. You have a role to play, concentrate on that. Go to the party. Watch the girl. Bring me the laptop. We roll out of here by the end of summer."

"That soon?" I ask.

"We won't be here another winter," my father vows. "If this works, we can find your mother. We can be a family again."

He's letting his crazy show through. I want to help my mom, of course.

"But what if she's working for them?" I ask him.

"Then she'll pay," he says quietly and I shiver inside. On the outside I school my face and slip the device into my pocket.

"The girl will need to wear something. Grab some clothes from down the hall." There's a cache for extra stuff. I picture Ami in one of the dresses the women wear around here and cringe a little. It's not her, but I know what he means. There's no way she'll pass for an innocent girlfriend without a makeover. I'll go to her house early tomorrow and we'll figure this out.

The laptop is stored on the roof. I can't believe this.

NEW YORK TIMES *LETTERS TO THE EDITOR*

MAY 14, 2021

Parents have been waiting anxiously for the coronavirus vaccine to be ready for use in children. I was happy to see the vaccine rolled out to teens ("US Vaccine Rollout Expands to Children Ages 12 to 15"). Those of us with elementary-age kids are still waiting but we hope the vaccine will be available to all soon.

The covid vaccine has been a modern miracle. Research groups, drug companies, governments, pharmacies, and doctors all working together to save lives. The People Against Violence Party is asking Americans to consider what else could be done together to save lives.

If this medicine can be created and shipped to people all over the country, could guns and other weapons be collected from all over the US and recycled or repurposed? Wouldn't that save as many lives as the vaccine?

Let's invest our time and money into saving lives and make the US the safest country in the world. Creating and selling guns has already been stopped, and many guns have been collected through buybacks.

We must expand this project by collecting all guns still privately owned in our country. Owners cooperate will receive generous payouts through the buyback. Those who refuse confiscation will have certain rights revoked in the interest of public safety. Let your representatives know you support the Swords Into Plowshares bill before Congress today.

Sincerely,
Mikayla Adamson
Baltimore, Maryland
People Against Violence

27

AMITY

IT FEELS different walking in Spenard on Saturday morning. The sun is high and bright. This is the first time the air in Anchorage has a warm, heavy quality I recognize from Baltimore.

My hair is a little damp and it feels good, cool on my head with the warm heat.

There are old strip malls on either side of the wide street I walk on. People are living in most of the buildings. Their faces are grim.

I'm reminded of history, of photos of people on the streets of Baltimore. Everyone in Maryland these days has a cared for, polished look. These folks are hungry, and I shiver as I pass them.

I still have Vale's hat. I'm wearing it again today. It smells faintly of pine and chlorine. I pull it low over my eyes. Everyone looks away from me when I glance around, but I notice a couple of kids playing with a broken shovel in front of a storefront that says Jewelers but clearly doesn't sell jewelry anymore.

They stare at me like I'm something they haven't seen before, and I slowly realize that most of the folks standing around are men, and the few women I see are shrinking back. The phrase "barefoot and pregnant" pops into my head, something else I remember from history. I give a little girl a wink and she cowers back.

When I get back to the trailer I go straight into my room. I sit on my bed, thinking. Tonight I'll go to the solstice party with Vale and pretend to be his girlfriend. My face twists. Maybe I should have paid more attention to the women lurking in the shadows. Is that what he'll expect from me?

I think back to the depo train. Everything felt totally new, there was so much I had never seen before. I realize how sheltered I was growing up in Baltimore and I wonder why we didn't travel more as a family, go to other places.

Surely it wasn't dangerous for us to visit New England, or the Midwest? Both territories signed the Universal Accord and purged their weapons.

I have a lot of questions. I wish I could travel around and talk to more people, find things out, understand what's going on in the world.

My phone buzzes, bringing me back to the gray walls around me. I hear a cupboard slam in the other room, Ren must be here. I instinctively tense up; I don't want Ren to know about my communications with my "mom."

I wish I knew whether it was my mom on the other side. The words don't sound like her, but that might be on purpose.

The phone buzzes again and I flop back on the bed.

> Hi honey how's it going?

Again with the honey stuff.

> Good. I'm meeting up with a friend later today.

Who's that?

> Vale Adamson. We're going to a party together for the solstice.

The phone buzzes in my hand and it says secure video call. This hasn't happened before. I glance toward the door where I still hear Ren moving around in the common area.

I swipe the screen and a picture appears—my mother and another woman stare out at me from the phone. I feel a pang when I realize my mom was there on the other side of the phone all along. The other part of the screen shows me —there must be a camera facing me from the phone.

I look different, my cheeks are red from the June sun. My hair is damp and short, hanging around my face and brushing my shoulders.

"What's happening, Amity?" my mom asks, her voice steady, not warm.

"I'm going to a party with Vale."

My mom nods eagerly. "Isaiah's son. The Society is aware of them."

"Mom, I saw Zeph, he came here, but he doesn't want to leave," I tell her. There's guilt dropping into my stomach at the thought. I worry that there's more I should have done for Zeph.

"Don't worry about Zeph. I'm sure he's fine," the other woman says.

My mom cuts in. "What else, Amity? What is happening at the party?"

"We're supposed to steal something," I tell them. I wonder how private this call is. "I'm not sure if I should..."

"This is a secure link," my mother tells me. "Tell us what you're supposed to steal."

"Me and Vale. We're supposed to steal a laptop that has information about the Peaceful Society that the Forge wants. We find the laptop and bring it to them."

My mom and the other woman exchange a glance. This has happened my whole life. At home, at school, and out in the community. My mom and the other CSOs: always whispering, giving each other significant looks.

I'm annoyed. Here I am, in Alaska, ready to risk my neck.

"*What?*" I say, pointedly.

My mom stares back at me, cold now.

"What, Mom? Can you fill me in, please? You said the link was secure," I add a little petulantly, even though I try not to. "I deserve to know."

My mother's lips purse. The other woman starts to speak, and apparently she's allowed to tell me what my own mother can't or won't.

"We believe the Forge is preparing to move to a location much closer to the Peaceful Society. There are reports of a site being prepared in West Virginia."

"Zeph said something about that, that they were going to try to negotiate with the PS," I tell them.

"Nonsense. We believe they are getting ready to strike the Peaceful Society, organize an attack that will cause widespread injuries or destruction. It could be plans for our electrical grid, something to take down our servers, or even a biological agent or poison."

I suddenly remember the trucks and buses. "There were trucks, so many trucks, lined up outside the building. And buses."

"What were they doing?" my mom asks, urgently. "Were they loading them?"

"Walking up and down." I picture the scene in my head, what I saw before Vale whisked me away. "They were checking them, inspecting maybe. I don't think Vale wanted me to see."

"I'm sure he didn't," the other woman says.

"Ami, we need that laptop. We need to know what they're planning, to prevent the Forge from terrorism."

Terrorism? That's not how I see Vale at all. I think of him: protecting me, laughing with me and teasing me, swimming powerfully beside me in the pool.

"Go with him tonight and get the laptop, but you must keep it away from the Forge. We can tell you where to drop it off later." My anxiety spikes at my mother's words.

My mother sees me breathing in, a sharp double breath, and knows what I'm up to. "Ami, listen. It's going to be okay. Do this and then you'll be done. We'll make arrangements to get you back here and you can start training with the other girls."

"Why me?" I can't help asking.

"The boy, he cares about you, right? He trusts you?"

Does she mean Zeph? He still cares about me, but I don't think he'll ever want to go back to the PS unless things change. But Vale's father keeps dangling him, using him to control me. Cooperate and we'll help Zeph. Cross us and he'll struggle.

"Vale," my mom clarifies.

"Oh. Yeah, I think so," I say, my eyes shifting.

"It's okay," she reassures me. "You're doing great. Getting close to him is an excellent strategy. There's no way they would involve you so quickly in the work of the Forge otherwise."

There's a knock on my door and I have a fleeting sense of relief. I don't want to know any more. I don't want to know if Vale is planning to do something terrible to the PS.

"Hey, Ami?" Ren pokes their head in. I try not to twist the phone away immediately. It's already angled towards the wall.

"Yeah, Ren?"

"I'm going next door to see if they need help with lunch. Want to come?" My eyes travel around the room, skimming over the phone. The link has been shut down. My mom is gone.

A message pops up.

> We will get you info for a secure location where you can drop off the equipment.
>
> Love you, honey.

28

AMITY

I HAVE butterflies all afternoon while Ren flits around the main house, working on a project to put new windows in. I'm glad it's warm out today.

By evening the banging of the hammer is so loud I head over to the trailer to hide in my room. There's no more word from the PS so I lie on my bed and stare at the ceiling, faded and grubby.

I'm not equipped for this mission, or anything else we're doing tonight. I have two knives now, that I bought at the market, but still no training in how to use them.

I'm better off with the self-defense skills we practiced at school. Our instructor emphasized how vital it is to protect yourself and your friends. But we mostly ignored her. I'm lucky I tried because that's what I do. I'm a trier. I like to do a good job. I like to please my teachers.

So here I am. Just stick me on a depo train and send me out into the world with nothing but money and highly sketchy instructions for getting to Anchorage and spying on the Forge.

I stare at the ceiling some more, thinking about it all, when I hear voices through the window. They're coming from the main house. Two low voices, and one of them is Vale.

I hurry out of bed, grabbing a brush to run it through my hair. I'm dressed in dark jeans and one of the T-shirts I've been wearing around. Hopefully this will work for the party we're going to. I have a feeling it won't be like a PS party. I hardly ever went to them anyway.

When I get to the main house Eli is there. I haven't seen him in a couple days. He's working on the revolution at all hours of the day and night, apparently.

At the moment he's spouting off about authoritarianism masquerading as harmony, and the uses of destabilizing insubordination.

"Eli." I turn, seeing Ren and Vale. Vale is on this side of the empty window frame, and Ren is on the outside.

I laugh. Ren put Vale to work installing our windows.

"And you have to remember that the consolidation of power ensures that the parameters of existence are dictated by the elite," Eli lectures Vale.

I don't know Eli well enough to ask him to leave Vale alone, but Ren jumps in.

"Eli. Give the man a break, he just got here."

"Hi, Ami," Vale says, scraping the exposed wood. Ren is pulling off old pieces of the sash and liner.

"Just a second, let me get this," they grunt at Vale, pulling a long strip of wood from the side of the window frame.

Sorry, I mouth to Vale and he shrugs helplessly. At the Forge he's in charge, son of the king. Here he's free labor, apparently.

"Ami, can we talk someplace?" Vale asks.

"Hang on there, handsome," Ren cuts in and I bite back a smile. "One more in the back."

"It's okay," I tell Vale as he follows to scrape another frame for Ren.

Eli and Qilan are chopping vegetables in the kitchen and I offer to help. Eli is talking a mile a minute but Qilan is quiet, watching me.

"You're going off with him?" she asks me.

"Yeah. To a solstice party?" I say it like a question.

Qilan's forehead wrinkles. "Where?" she asks.

"At the Brotherhood."

Even Eli stops talking to stare at me. "I hope you have a good reason. You're going with him?"

"He was invited," I say defensively. "I'm just going along as a...guest."

Qilan snorts and together they start shoveling vegetables into a pot. She and Eli exchange a wry look.

"You can stay home, you know," she offers. "We'll be around. We might watch an old movie with the projector or something."

That sounds more my speed than a party, for sure. "I said I'd go," I deflect.

Vale comes back with Ren.

"There's His Highness now," Eli announces.

"Eli," I chide him. The distrust radiates off of Qilan, but I wasn't expecting that from Eli. Vale is unbothered. Fair enough. He turns to me.

"So, can we talk somewhere?"

I shyly lead him out the back door and over to the trailer. It's old and shabby, despite the work Ren has been doing to fix things up, but it's no worse than most of the places around the neighborhood. We go into my room and I shut the door, immediately thinking about being in his room at the Forge.

"I can't take you swimming," I joke nervously. "The pool's closed."

"That's okay," Vale says. "I got to help with the windows." And he has a small, secret smile.

He swings his backpack off his back and unzips it.

"I brought these for you. It's clothes for the party."

I eye the pile mistrustfully. It's not very big. I glance up and he immediately guesses the source of my hesitation.

"I think you look great, just like that. But the girls at the party will be wearing skirts and stuff, and we need to blend in as much as we can."

I nod, moving over to the bed and the clothes. There's a shirt in a soft material with a scoop neck that's red and he brought a skirt. I think that's what it is. It's narrow and black.

"How do you walk in it?" I ask, holding it up. Vale grimaces.

"I think it's stretchy." He reaches out to pull on the fabric and show me. "We can bring your clothes in my bag," he explains. "At least a pair of jeans. But this is probably best for getting in to the party." His eyes dart around.

I sigh. He's right. Most of the women I see up here, even Qilan, wear skirts. I haven't worn a skirt in years.

They aren't exactly against the rules to wear in the PS but definitely frowned upon.

"What about my shoes?" I glance down at the black boots I'm wearing.

"Those are good."

What happens next, I put the clothes on? I shudder at the thought of wearing them over at the house and hearing what Ren and Qilan and Eli have to say.

"Uh, should we go over the plan?" Vale asks. He's not in a big hurry. He seems nervous. Maybe I need to be the one to hold things together.

"Come here," I invite and we both sit on the bed. I take a deep breath. "Okay, what are you thinking?"

I listen carefully while he tells me about where the laptop is, in storage on the roof of the building. I nod, wishing I knew more about the Brotherhood so I could be more help. I memorize what he says so I can act as naturally as possible when I'm there. Focus on the job.

Vale starts to close his backpack, then looks up. "Anything else I should pack? A phone or anything? There aren't any pockets," he says apologetically.

"No pockets?" I laugh. "Wait, are you serious?"

He shrugs.

"I'll bring my phone and stuff in my purse." I show him the purse I picked up at the market and he nods; apparently it passes his inspection. And stuff meaning my knife, since that's better than leaving it at home and wishing I had it.

"Okay, I'll just—" I pick up the clothes. Vale's eyes are glued to the floor suddenly.

"Could you step out?" I ask shyly.

"Of course, sorry, Ami." Vale shakes his head as if to

clear it and springs to his feet, his tall form ducking through the doorway and pulling the door shut. I change into the red top, giving a side eye to the way it hugs my shape.

Then I slide into the skirt, which is stretchy as he promised. The skirt is short, or I'm tall, and a sliver of tan skin shows between the bottom of the shirt and the top of the skirt. I try pulling up the skirt but now it's too short to be comfortable. I pull it back down and poke my head out.

"Almost ready," I tell him when he glances up from the folding chair he's sitting in. "Come here a second, I need to ask you something."

He comes immediately. I sit him on the bed and show him.

"I'm not sure if I should wear the skirt lower, but it leaves a gap here, or higher, but then it's so short?" I ask, tugging the skirt up to show him.

"Vale?"

His eyes are on my legs. They seem a little glassy.

"Vale? The skirt?"

"Um…" He looks up to my face, grimacing.

"Sorry. Sorry, Ami. What was the question again?"

I sigh. "What do I do about this skirt?" I show him again. He starts to reach out and pauses before his hands touch me.

"May I?"

Suddenly my mouth is as dry as it's ever been. His voice is so intimate, and his hands are hovering over my hips. I can't form the word yes so I nod, holding his eyes. Without breaking my gaze he brings his hands to my hips, tugging the skirt lower, leaving that sliver of stomach.

His hands linger on my hips as he says thickly, "Like this, I think."

I'm silent for a beat and his hands are still on my hips. I wonder what it would be like for his hands to slide around my waist, pulling me towards him. As if in answer to my thought his grip slides up, resting on the skin between my red shirt and the tight black skirt.

"Ami, I..."

I bring my hands to his shoulders and he pulls me even closer, hugging me between his legs. His breathing is deep, he sounds like he's trying to calm himself down.

"I'm worried about tonight," he mutters. "I don't want anything to happen to you."

Oh. He's worried about me. I thought maybe we were going to kiss. I hug him.

"It's okay," I reassure him. Maybe seeing me in these clothes makes me seem vulnerable. "It's what I want. I want to get the laptop," I tell him. The words are heavy and wrong in my mouth. I do want to get the laptop, but I'm speaking a half-truth.

"This is something I need to do," I tell him. At least that's the truth. We stand there, hugging, as his breathing regulates. Then he releases me and I back up, giving him space to stand. He busies himself with the backpack, and I grab what I need for my purse.

It occurs to me that I might not see Vale after tonight. If I can get that laptop for the PS, and get it to a drop point tomorrow, they said I'd be on my way back soon. And Vale will be here, in Anchorage.

When he turns back I slip closer and he stills. I may

never see him after tonight. I bring my lips close to his, almost brushing them together.

"Vale, can we…"

He closes the space between us and our mouths press softly, our lips fitting together. He's gentle. His lips are soft.

There's a thud of the backpack hitting the floor and Vale's hands are gripping my ribcage, pulling me closer. I angle my head, exploring, and drop my purse to wind my arms around his neck.

My whole body tingles. I'm hot all over but the kiss is slow, gentle, and ends too soon. I step back, and he drops his hands awkwardly.

Then I remember I'm supposed to be his girlfriend at the party.

"Okay." I take a couple of breaths, backing up more, trying to remember what we were doing. "So. We're going together, like we're on a date?"

"Yeah," Vale says slowly. "But we don't have to do what everyone else is doing," he goes on, looking worried.

"What kind of party are we talking about?" I joke.

"Oh, not like that, but guys are pretty protective of their women up here. You'll want to stay close…" He trails off, suddenly unsure again.

"That's okay. Yeah." This party is going to be quite the experience, I can tell already.

29

AMITY

RATHER THAN GO through the house and get sucked into another home improvement project, we cut through the side yard.

"Ami," Ren calls, hurrying off the porch. I brace myself to say no to more window hanging, but they gently pull me aside and slip something into my hand.

"What's this?" I feel a small piece of paper, folded twice.

"My brother's name and the name of the camp," Ren whispers to me.

"Ren—" I start but Ren cuts me off with another whisper.

"I'll be honest, kiddo. I have a bad feeling about this." Their eyes sweep up my girlfriend clothes. "If something happens and you don't come back, if you end up back in the PS...well, he needs help. If there's anything you can do..." they trail off.

I gaze at Ren steadily, thinking they may have guessed more than they let on this whole time. Then I swallow.

"I'll be back in a couple hours, Ren," I assure them and try to hand the paper back. Ren pushes my hand away.

"Ami, please, I've tried to help you. If you have the chance—"

"Of course," I reassure them, giving Ren a quick hug. "If I have the chance to help him, of course I will."

I turn and Vale is waiting. Without comment he turns south, away from the Forge. I follow, glad for my boots at least, and that it's warm enough I'm not shivering in this outfit.

When we get out to the main road, it's still bright outside. The sun hovers over the horizon. Vale holds his hand out. I take it and we hold hands. He's wearing jeans and a T-shirt, his backpack slung on his back. I'm in this get-up trying to figure out the trick to walking in a skirt.

There's a car waiting by the side of the road and Vale heads straight for it. It's one of the old cars they have up here, with an engine that makes a lot of noise. It smells too, the exhaust. This one is shiny and black. We slide into the back and a man I've never seen before is driving. He and Vale exchange a glance and the car starts.

I settle into my seat, not sure what I should say in front of the driver, who Vale has not introduced.

"Your seatbelt," Vale says to me quietly.

"Where?" I check around. He's looking at something behind me.

"Put your seatbelt on, Ami," he grumbles. The driver turns a sharp corner and I slide on the seat, leaning to regain my balance. It's different from the slow, self-driving cars and e-buses back in the PS. I poke my hand down around the seat, feeling for a safety belt.

Vale blows out an exasperated breath and scoots over in the seat, right next to me, his leg pressed against mine. Then he reaches over me.

"Vale," I protest and press my back against the back seat of the car. His face comes closer and closer to me. I can't stop thinking about the kiss, but I notice the driver's eyes are flicking to the rearview mirror.

Vale grabs something next to my ear, pulling a strap across my body and under my other arm. There's a clip next to my hip that he grabs with his other hand and he clips them together. Then he takes my hand.

"This button releases it," he says, touching my fingers to the clip.

I roll my eyes. *Clearly.*

"All safe now." He sounds pleased.

A little shy to look him directly in the eye, still hovering over me, I half close my eyes and watch him in my periphery. He tugs the belt once, twice. I'm strapped in tight now. Then he moves back to his side of the car. When I glance over, he's still watching me.

"You need to wear your seatbelt up here," is all he says. The man driving is glancing curiously in the rearview mirror but Vale says nothing else, only reaches over to take my hand again. Is he nervous? His hand is warm in mine. My stomach growls and I realize I didn't eat dinner.

The car turns onto a crowded road. There are lots of cars and trucks waiting in line, and people grouped everywhere. A crowd, in clusters, is waiting to go through a door. Most of them are men but I see a few women scattered around. I'm glad Vale brought these clothes for me. I would have stood out in my other stuff. The girls are dressed like me, in dresses and skirts.

I cringe a little. They look so helpless. How can they defend themselves in these outfits? I shudder, thinking that the women up here seem so vulnerable, there's no other way to describe it. They don't look strong; it's like they don't train at all. I think of the weightlifting classes back home, the hours with the swim team.

My mom says our Peace is not a product of weakness, that women had to become strong enough to demand it. It's for these women I need to follow through with the orders from the PS, even if it means I won't see Vale again.

When the car stops I fiddle with the seatbelt. Vale opens his door while I'm untangling myself.

"Sit tight a second," he tells me.

So I do, wondering why he's out of the car and I'm not. I hug my purse.

My door opens and it's Vale reaching in, holding out his hand, and I take it. He pulls me out and it reminds me of a scene from an old video. He holds my hand tight, poking his head in to say something low to the driver before shutting the door. The driver leaves and we are standing on the sidewalk outside the tall brick wall of a building.

Vale pulls me closer, tucking me under his arm.

"Here we are. We'll go in, look around, get you something to eat, and relax for a bit." He glances at his watch. "It's not even midnight."

I nod tightly and focus on my job. I need to watch out for any danger we might be in, and I need to copy the other girls.

Next to us the line snakes down the block. I see girls tucked under men's arms as I am. I mimic their body language. A little timid, a little wary, eyes down.

Feeling the shift, Vale turns, speaking into the hair hanging around my face.

"Good," he murmurs. He leads up to the line at the door where a couple of large guards stand, along with a tan, blond man with a distasteful expression on his face. The man wears a gun strapped to the front of his shirt and I look everywhere but at the gun.

Vale has one I think, and knows how to shoot. But after everything MAV went through, my family went through, it's crazy to see the gun casually there. Like my grandmother and all the other martyrs' deaths mean nothing. It only strengthens my resolve.

Vale will be okay. I'll get the laptop and get it to the PS. That will keep Greater Maryland safe from whatever the Forge is planning. Vale can go back to whatever he was doing before this.

I might as well enjoy myself. I cuddle in closer, squeezing his waist.

The blond man interrupts my train of thought.

"Hey, man. Thanks for coming." He reaches forward a hand and Vale clasps it with his free hand. Then they're stuck in the handshake. "Didn't know if I'd see you here, Adamson."

"Jeremy. Here I am," Vale says in a harder voice than I've heard him use.

"I didn't hear back," Jeremy says, fishing for information.

"My girl wants to celebrate," Vale says, giving me a

225

squeeze, "so here we are." The blond man's eyes slide up and down me. It's gross. I imagine his body crumpling, stunned by CSOs.

Behind our conversation, the guards are scanning phones and watches, letting people in.

"And who's this?" The man, Jeremy, steps closer.

"This is Ami. Ami, Jeremy," Vale says smoothly.

I go against my instinct and shrink back, pretending to be intimidated by Jeremy. "Nice to meet you."

"Well, let me know if you need anything," Jeremy says, his eyes lingering even as he turns to enter the building.

We duck through the door after him and it's crowded. There are people everywhere. Loud music thumps, the bass vibrating through me. I stay close to Vale and let him lead me through the crowd.

There's a lot of movement on the other side of the room where people are dancing and a live band is playing music on a roughly built stage. The ceiling seems impossibly high —maybe this was an old warehouse before the Integration? The walls are rough brick and it's huge. Already I'm wondering about being on the roof, four or five stories up.

Vale remembers I'm hungry, so our first stop is a table covered with a spread of delicious-looking food.

"Fill it up," he directs, handing me a plate.

"I intend to," I tell him.

When the plate is full I hold it carefully with two hands. Vale's arm is still wrapped around my waist, and he leads me toward a door on the side of the room. We push through another crowd and duck out the door.

There's an old, fenced parking lot with tables and chairs and benches out here. The sun is a deep brilliant gold, just starting to set finally, and the sky is washed over in fiery orange. Vale pulls me over to a bench. Before we get there a man comes up to us and tries to start a conversation. Vale dismisses him, telling the man he has to take care of his "girl." Once we're sitting on the bench, Vale sighs.

"You can talk to him if you want to," I tell him. "You don't have to 'take care of' me."

Vale laughs. "I don't want to talk to any of these idiots. They're just trying to get information on the Forge. They're watching us, trying to figure out why I came tonight."

"Is the Forge having a party for the solstice?" I ask.

"Not this year." Vale's face is masked.

That's right, they're getting ready to move, so maybe they don't have time to throw a party. Another man sidles up to us.

"Hey, Adamson, how's it going?"

"Get out of here," Vale grumbles, his patience breaking. "I'm busy." The man startles and with an apologetic look Vale scoops me up and into his lap. The man gives him a knowing grin and slips off.

"Vale," I complain lightly, laughing.

"Just eat your food, Ami." He ducks his head next to mine. "This might give us a minute of privacy." He ducks lower and his lips brush against my ear, by accident. "Are you okay?"

"Sure," I tell him. "He left, so...should I get off?"

30

AMITY

"No, stay here."

I sit in Vale's lap, eating the food. There's a shout nearby and a man staggers past. He's followed by a couple other guys, alternately cussing the man out and trying to help him get to a place to sit down.

I find myself burrowing deeper. Vale's grip tightens around my waist, and I feel his arm as firm as the seatbelt was in the car. Even though he's only holding me in place, it feels incredibly intimate.

I close my eyes briefly, enjoying the touch of his skin against mine.

"Vale Adamson. What've you got there?" Much closer this time, another drunk guy. Is this what all their parties are like up here?

"If you don't turn around right now you're not going to walk out of here tonight," Vale doesn't raise his voice but his words jolt me. I'm not used to threats, which are banned in the PS. Vale's trying to get rid of the guy, and it works. He lurches off to bother someone else.

"Finish up, Ami. Then we'll look around." His eyes slide to the brick wall we're sitting next to. According to the Forge, secure storage for the Brotherhood is in a security office on the roof.

They weren't able to tell us whether there was indoor access—that's part of what we need to check around and find out. We know there's a fire escape on the back of the building, around the corner from where we are. I'd rather not take a super-exposed route to the roof if I don't have to. Especially since it won't be getting completely dark tonight, only fading to civil twilight.

I'm done and we stand up. Vale stays glued to my side.

"Let's head back inside. We can be seen as a couple and take a look around, see if we can find out anything about indoor access," Vale tells me.

One idea is to check the elevator, but I'm not sure what excuse we have for using it. I'm already tired thinking about climbing up stairs or a ladder to get all the way up five floors. In an ideal world, we could get on the elevator and press R for roof and go straight there.

But nothing in Anchorage is ideal. I realize that now. I wonder if Zeph has come to the same realization. I might not see him before I leave. It no longer feels like he needs to be rescued. I guess he'll be staying here, training, and I'll be back in the PS, training for HighClear. It's like we're joining different sides in a war.

That's silly. The PS is strictly against war. They will do what they have to, disarm the men from the Forge if they attack, but they would never kill anyone, right?

Then there's the Forge soldiers. I'm not sure they even

know what they want. Do they really want things to go back to how they were, with people shooting each other in the face, with men forced to serve in wars and die halfway across the world? I wish I could talk to Vale about it more. He seems...reasonable, intelligent.

Remember your mission, Ami, I have to remind myself. Get the laptop, contact the PS, drop it off, and go home. Vale's got the backpack, our means of transporting the laptop. I'll have to get away with the backpack somehow. My mind draws a blank when I try to imagine it, but I'll figure something out. I'll have to.

"What about the fire escape, should we take a look?" I ask, before we enter the building again.

Vale hesitates, thinking. "We don't want to be seen hanging around it. Let's leave it for now."

He takes my hand and leads me inside. There's a bar and someone is getting drinks for the men who cluster around it.

"Do you want anything to drink?" Vale asks me.

"Oh, I don't drink alcohol."

"I figured." Is he making fun of me? "Soda water?"

"No, I'm good."

"Okay." Vale's scanning the room. "Let's head over there." He nods towards the dance floor. He squints at the band up on the stage. "I know the bass player, actually. Let's say hi to him after this song and maybe we can take a look backstage."

"Okay." Dancing. How hard can that be?

We slide through the bodies. There's more of a mix of men and women on the dance floor. My eyes widen at how close they are dancing; plenty of couples are plastered together. Vale leads me close to the band and draws me in.

"Is this okay?" he says into my ear. The music is loud and pumping through me like blood.

I nod, peeking at him. He has a smile as he pulls me all the way against him and we sway, pressed against each other. People brush against us but he keeps his arms tight around me, turning us away from the wilder dancers, burying his face in my hair.

"Vale." I tilt my head up to speak in his ear. No one can hear us over the sound of the band. "Is this really part of the mission? Dancing?"

"Ami." He stares into my face, then ducks down, his lips against my ear. "I've wanted to do this since I first saw you at that courthouse."

"No way," I joke automatically. He tightens his grip in response, one hand sliding up my back, the other sliding lower, pulling me against him.

"It's true," he says, turning us again. "You were so different from how I remember you."

I tip my head back to answer him. "So are you. Different."

His smile grows a shade cocky. "In a good way?"

"Maybe. But I could tell you were up to no good," I say, sticking with the truth.

"I wouldn't have taken you for a girl who likes a bad boy," he teases me.

"Shut up," I say, shoving down the conflicting feelings that are bubbling up. I feel close to him, I trust him. Like he knows me, and knows parts of me that no one back home took the time to notice.

How am I going to leave him after this? I wonder if there's a way I can still see him again. Maybe I'll get sent on another mission to Anchorage? Or we can meet up somewhere in the Midwest?

But what will he think of me after tonight? He'll think I'm a traitor, dishonest. He'll think I was tricking him all along.

In a way I was, but so much of this didn't feel like a trick. Our chats in the alley outside the market, him finding me there every day. Swimming together, dancing in this sweaty crowd. None of it feels like a trick.

The song ends too soon and Vale starts to tug me again, heading for the stage. The band is putting their instruments down and getting ready to take a break. Vale waves to one of the guys, his friend I guess, who waves back and motions to the side of the stage.

I stay close as we head there, and look all around, scanning the area behind the stage.

"Vale!" The guy spreads his arms for a hug and Vale lets go of me for a second to give his friend a bear hug before drawing me back, sliding his arm around my waist.

"This is my girlfriend, Ami." My stomach flops over at the words.

The bass player smiles at me, genuine. "Nice to meet you, Vale's girlfriend."

"Ami," Vale corrects. Then he cringes a little. "Hey, it's super loud."

"Yeah," the guy agrees. "We're heading up to take our break, want to come?"

That's exactly what we wanted.

"Sure," Vale says. "Let's go catch up."

"Come on." The guy shouts introductions to the rest of the band, including Vale's last name, which gets a reaction. Everyone seems to know about his dad and the Forge. Soon we're all cramming into an elevator to go up to the "green room."

I check out the buttons on the elevator: 1, 2, 3, 4, and basement. Okay, so no roof. But there must be a way up there from the fourth floor, right? The guy punches three and we all crowd in as the doors shut and we head up to the third floor.

The green room turns out to be an old lounge of dusty couches and coolers full of beer. Vale accepts one for him, nothing for me, and pretends to drink. We cuddle on one of the couches and chitchat with the guys in the band. Vale talks to them about coming to the Forge to play for a party there, and they're excited to line up another gig.

I wait until they're all engrossed in conversation and then stand up. Five pairs of eyes find me.

"Sorry. I'm just gonna find a restroom. I'll be right back."

"You okay on your own, babe?" Vale asks.

Babe? I want to answer *of course,* or maybe *don't call me babe,* but I can't be out of my character, the shy and retiring girlfriend of Vale Adamson. "Oh—uh, yeah. I saw it in the hall. You stay here, I'll just be a minute."

"Okay." He and the guys settle back and keep talking about the gig. Vale's eyes are on me as I tug my skirt, adjusting it down, and walk toward the door. Maybe I can find a stairwell.

I close the door behind me. I really did see a bathroom between here and the elevator, but I don't need to use it. What I'd like is to see where the other doors lead, and find the stairwell. I'm wandering down to the end of the hall when I find a heavier door. Through the narrow window I see a set of stairs. *Bingo!*

31

AMITY

I GIVE the handle an experimental pull, and the door opens smoothly. I poke my head into the stairwell, listening. There's no sound, so I slip through the door and look up, my eyes taking in the stairs leading up another floor and beyond.

Then I hear a soft click behind me. It's not what I was expecting to hear. I turn around and check—the door is locked!

Shoot. I don't want to rattle it too much but I tug a couple times and it stays resolutely shut. Now I see the card slider to the right of the door.

I check for security cameras, but there are none. I'm not exactly practiced at covert missions. I look longingly down the stairs. Every instinct is telling me to go down, search for a way out of here. What's Vale going to do if I don't come back?

But here I am, and I can see the landing for the fourth floor above me. I climb the stairs quietly and turn to where the stairs keep going up. This must be the roof access we were looking for! Maybe I can get the laptop now. But where would I put it? All I have is my little purse. I continue climbing up.

The stairs are narrow above the fourth-floor landing, the railing a rough metal rather than the smooth wooden balustrade from below. A small landing greets me at the top, the floor dingy. There's an old metal door with a push bar to open. I stop to listen but hear nothing, so I push the bar in and press into the door.

It moves half an inch and then stops, held by a deadbolt. Now I see it, a keyhole and the thin sliver of the metal bolt holding the door in place.

Frustrated, I push the door a couple more times and then begin searching the walls around the door. Maybe the key is stored around here somewhere?

The walls are rough brick, and there's nothing. No sign of a key, no instructions, nothing posted anywhere. I search my purse for something that might help but I don't have anything like a hairpin, not that I would know how to unlock a door with that anyway. I think it only happens in books.

Frustrated, I rattle the door one more time and start back down the stairs. Maybe Vale will have a better idea of how we can get through.

At the fourth floor I carefully try the door, but it's locked with a card swipe, same as the third floor. I try each door until I get to the first floor, which is also locked.

What am I going to do now? There are a few stairs to my left that lead down to a door to the outside, I assume. It's a double door made of metal, for deliveries maybe?

That wouldn't be unlocked, right? I twist the knob, push, then sigh with relief when the door slides open.

Noise greets me. I enter directly into the parking lot where I sat with Vale earlier.

I quickly push the door shut behind me.

"Where did you come from?" someone asks me immediately.

"Bathroom," I lie and he seems to accept it. He's not wearing black like the Brotherhood guards.

"Oh." He stares at the doors.

I flit away. It's gotten rowdier out here, and I don't like being by myself. They've set up a ring in the parking lot, like for boxing, with sets of ropes ringing a raised platform.

Inside the ropes, two men with gloves circle each other. Around the ring there's throngs of people shouting and pushing to get to a place where they can see. I aim for the door to go back in. I think my best bet is to meet Vale when the band comes back down from upstairs.

I push through the crowded room, back to the dance floor. Music still plays through speakers; the band is not back yet. I get over to the side of the stage where the elevators are. There are a couple of Brotherhood guards standing around the elevator and the exits over here.

While I'm trying to figure out if I should go back upstairs to Vale, the elevator door opens.

The band exits, with two other people coming behind: Vale, with his hands bound behind his back, and a Brotherhood guard.

I hesitate, not sure what to do, then decide to play dumb.

"Vale, there you are, I couldn't find you," I wail, coming up to him. "What's going on?" I ask the guard.

They all look at me.

"Ami, where did you go?" Vale asks, his voice raised.

"I—I got confused." I try to appear confused. "I went to the bathroom, then I thought we were meeting down here, but I couldn't find you." I turn big eyes on the guard, who is rolling his eyes at the band.

"Dude, your girlfriend's dumb."

Vale stiffens. But I give him an awkward hug. His wrists are in a zip tie behind his back.

"I'm so glad I found you, I want to dance." I pout a little. Vale glares at the guard, who narrows his eyes.

"She was down here, man, I was just trying to find her," Vale says with quiet authority.

"Yeah, she did go to the bathroom," the band chimes in, supporting Vale.

The guard brings a knife from his belt and cuts the zip tie and Vale pulls me close. The guard doesn't apologize.

"Stay down here." He looks from Vale to me. "No more going upstairs." He glares at the band.

"Sorry, of course. We didn't know." The leader of the band is conciliatory.

"Come on." Vale leads me away onto the dance floor, which is less crowded without live music, and pulls me close.

"I found the indoor roof access, I think," I tell him. "Above the fourth floor, a landing and a door, but it was locked. We need a key. I'm so sorry I couldn't get back, the stairwell was locked and I couldn't get through without a card."

Vale visibly relaxes. "What did you do?"

"I came out the delivery entrance."

He grins. "Okay. Well, here we are, but I think they're watching us now."

I let my eyes dart around the room and I see he's right, the Brotherhood guards have their eyes on us.

"What are we going to do?" I muse. "How can we find the key and get up there?"

"We'll have to use the outside access," Vale says. "Come on, let's take a look."

We weave through the crowd and make our way outside, in time for a big, ragged cheer from the people crushed around the boxing ring. Vale and I slip over to the bench we sat on earlier and huddle together.

"There's so many people," I say, unsure.

"They can be distracted," he tells me, glancing around, taking it in. "I think..." He trails off, then asks. "Do you think you could get up there by yourself? Climb to the roof and look for the laptop?"

"Of course." I nod.

"Okay. I can distract them." As he talks he slips the backpack off his shoulders.

I had expected us to work together: finding the rooftop office, breaking in, locating the correct device. But it looks like I'll be doing it by myself. *Maybe it's better this way*, I think. Maybe there's a way I can leave directly once I have it.

I see my pants, my other clothes, in the backpack and resolve to change as soon as I can, especially if I'm climbing a ladder that leads up to the top of the building.

"What are you going to do?" I ask, feeling anxious. He's not exactly a popular guy around here tonight.

"I'm going to get my workout in," he says, grinning, and walks off, leaving me with the backpack. I wait a minute, watching him push through the crowd and talk to one of the guys standing near the corner of the ring.

He's going to do something with the fight. As I'm looking over I hear the wet smack of a fist against a face and a big guy goes down in the ring, hitting the floor hard.

It jolts me, and I don't wait a second longer. I hurry inside and escape into the first women's bathroom I can find, changing into pants and pulling the dark leather jacket over my red shirt. I scrunch the skirt up and shove it into the backpack. I don't ever want to wear that again, but Vale did bring it for me and I shouldn't throw it away. I stuff my purse into the backpack, but I slip the paper from Ren into my pocket for safekeeping.

Now I work my way back outside, keeping my head down.

There's no one in the ring, but the crowd is growing, quieter than before. I'm glad it's twilight now. I definitely feel safer in these jeans with the dark coat. I am about to turn the corner to the back part of the building when two new guys duck under the ropes and into the ring and one of them is Vale.

Now I understand the growing crowd, every set of eyes on the ring. Vale's got boxing gloves on and a big guard from the Brotherhood is pulling on his own gloves, grinning. They've stripped off their shirts and the other guy is as wide as a brick wall.

Vale is tall and trim, his arms and shoulders wrapped in

muscle. I falter, unable to leave without knowing what happens. Does Vale know how to box? What is he going to do, let that guy beat him up?

The announcer is introducing the new fight and playing up the rival militias, talking about Vale and the Forge. With all eyes on the ring, I tear myself away and scoot around the corner. I tighten the backpack's straps, and prepare myself.

I'll have to jump and grab onto the first rung to pull myself onto the ladder. I glance around rapidly, but there's no one back here by the dumpsters. I bend my knees, launching myself in the air. Thank goodness for all my swimming and training back home.

My fingers brush the metal of the first rung, but I fall back before I can get a firm grasp on it. I crouch, readying myself, and spring again, preparing to grab as soon as I can grasp it. My fingers seize the rung and immediately I'm pulling, reaching for the rung above and tucking my body up. In a second I'm on the ladder, and I see that it truly is empty back here.

There's a roar from around the corner. I can't let myself be distracted. I look up, seeing the network of ladders that go up, up, above the fourth floor to the roof of the old factory building. I climb.

32

AMITY

When I was a little girl, my mom figured out that I was afraid of heights. She found me outside one day, sullenly refusing to climb a tree. The other kids were teasing me.

She didn't interfere, but afterward she talked to me about it, gently easing the secret out of me. I didn't want to tell her. I didn't want her to see me as weak or afraid.

I was right to be wary. That weekend and for years after she took me to the climbing gym.

"Maybe not today, maybe not next time," she'd say, looking up the long walls to the top. "But someday you are going to climb to the top, calmly, and then you'll know you have your fear under control."

I could barely climb the first couple holds that first day. She didn't coach me other than, "Climb as far as you can, and then just stay there. Get yourself under control." She didn't need to explain what that meant—we worked on it all the time at school.

"We had it all along," she mused to me one day at a café down the street from the climbing gym. I don't know how far I'd gotten at that point. Maybe halfway up? Definitely not to the top, that took years.

"What did we have?" I wanted to know.

"Women had the strength to change the world, to make it better." I remember her face, her passion. "We just weren't thinking big enough. We weren't thinking about what it means to put the public good first."

I'd heard the phrase public good before, and I knew it was connected to our Privileges.

"Like Rights and Privileges?" I asked.

"Exactly." Her eyes shone. "We let them take Rights way too far. No one has the right to put other people in danger. No one has the right to hurt people, not even the government."

"Not even the Peaceful Society?" I asked, thinking about our Officers in white.

"No. Violence is over. Everyone in MAV, including your grandmother, made sure of that. She would be so proud of you for working on this, conquering your fear."

I thought about my grandmother, who was always busy when I was a kid, always running around to MAV events and protests. They said she was part of the team at Tel Nof that disarmed the final nuclear weapons, that supported women throughout the Middle East to help them seize power and start recycling and repurposing their weaponry.

Every time I climbed after that, I thought about my grandmother. I pictured her in a city in the desert, organizing groups of women, helping them overcome their fear. I wanted to be like her.

I eventually climbed to the top. Even after, we'd still go back now and then for me to do that. Climb to the top. Breathe. Remind myself that I am in control of my fear.

I think of my grandmother as I climb the side of the building. It's me and this ladder, me and the height.

My heart pangs at the thought of leaving Vale behind. What if he gets hurt, fighting in there to cover for me?

I wonder what my mother really thinks about the way the PS handles men and Oath Refusers. I think I know what she would say—this is the way things are now, and it's that way for a reason. We all get to live a safe life, and that's the priority now because greed and violence were the priorities for so long before.

"Now we're trying this," I've heard her say, a little bit light, a little dismissive, when people question the wisdom of the PS leadership. But how long can you keep men under extra rules and restrictions, just for the sins of their fathers and grandfathers?

The thought of Vale in a PS ankle cuff, his eyes glassed over from meds, causes a deep, shaky hurt inside me. That's what they would do to him, what my mother would do to him. For the public good.

Maybe I can be part of changing that when I get older. Maybe I can help get more representation from men into leadership and address their concerns.

This ladder is higher than the top of the climbing wall, and I'm glad my legs and shoulders are strong. I'm not tired. I hear a wave of cheering as I reach the top and pull myself over, and wonder what it means.

Up here there are only a couple of parts that stick up on the wide, flat roof. There's a metal door in a little area that pokes up on its own that might be the stairway I found. I slip over to give a quick tug on the door but it's locked. So that won't be a way out.

Checking behind it, I see what I'm looking for. There's a small building up here, like a large shed. My eyes scan for cameras, but I don't see anything so I step quietly to the side, where there's a window.

My heart leaps. There's a man in a chair and he's facing me. However, his eyes are pointed up to something over the window, and it's darker out here than inside the room. He doesn't react to my quick peek. I move around to the other side so I can see what he's watching.

There are half a dozen monitors and I see laptops in a careless pile. I have the serial number of the laptop we need memorized. Everyone wants this laptop. Is it part of an evil plan the Forge has to attack the PS? Or does it hold PS secrets that the Forge wants to air?

I'll find out. I need to get in there and start looking at the serial numbers of those laptops. The man doesn't turn, just keeps watching the screens. I'm relieved there's not one showing the roof or the fire escape. They're all videos of the party downstairs, the front entrance where the line is still filing through, and the side parking lot where the fight is going on.

Even though I need to get on with this and figure out how to get into the room and get around this guy, my eyes snag on the image of Vale in his boxing gloves as he dances forward and back. He and the other guy look worse for wear. One of Vale's eyes is swollen shut. The other guy is dragging himself forward, but barely upright. Vale ducks his punches easily, swinging back with tight, controlled strikes. It's kind of beautiful to watch.

I don't know anything about boxing. It was banned along with all violent sports by the PS, but somehow Vale makes it look more like dancing than fighting with his head drifting side to side, his feet moving and twisting on the floor in neat, quick movements.

The guard reaches for a cup to take a drink and I shrink back. How am I going to get past him? Can I lure him out somehow? Cause a distraction on the roof he'll want to check out? The problem is there's not much up here, meaning he'll see me.

I watch as the guy stretches, grabs a couple things, and opens the door. I hover on the other side of the building, carefully tracking his movements. He moves off and lights a cigarette, wandering to the edge of the building to look down over the parking lot.

I can't believe my luck. I slip into the small room and start checking the backs of the laptops, trying to find the serial number we were given. It's not there, but I open drawers of the desk and there are more electronics. I glance out the window to check on the guard, but he's still smoking, standing a distance away.

Underneath a tablet I find it. The sleek gray laptop is unassuming but a sticker on the back has the serial number I've been looking for. I tuck it quickly into the backpack. I check the top screen for Vale's fight but the ring is empty. What happened?

My eyes dart around to the other screens trying to find him, but I don't see him anywhere. Does that mean he's behind the building? Is he on his way up here? I need to move quickly. I zip up the backpack and head for the door. Then I realize I haven't been keeping an eye on the guard.

A quick check tells me he's on his way back. I open the door as quietly as I can and hurry out, hoping he's not paying too much attention, that he can't see through the window to where I am. I'm not sure which part of the building to put between me and the guard, and I'm suddenly reminded of playing tag, or hide and seek, and trying to stay on one side of a tree or a couch.

There's a shout. I can't see what's going on, but when I hear pounding footsteps I skitter away around the side of the shack, office, whatever it is. Now I can see a bit through this window. The guard's headed back the way I came, around the entrance to the stairs and over to the back wall.

Is it Vale? Did Vale get up here already? Or is it someone from the Brotherhood? Did they figure out I'm up here? I crouch down and peer through, waiting for a sign of what's happening.

33

AMITY

I CAREFULLY STEP around the side of the small building, conscious that the laptop we need is in my backpack. The wind whips my hair and it's cooler now; I wish I'd brought Vale's hat. I should be searching for any other way off this roof. I try not to make noise stepping in the black gravel.

I can't see what's going on so I creep to the other side to check.

What I see feels like a punch in the stomach. The guard is holding his arms out straight, pointed at the edge of the roof, with a gun in his hands.

Vale appears from the ladder, pulling himself up. He rises slowly, his hands in the air. His left eye is still swollen shut but he's got his shirt back on and he looks okay besides that. They are talking but with the wind whipping up here I can't hear what they're saying.

I glance around again but there's nothing to see. The stairs are locked, but maybe the keys to the stairs are in the office.

I check on Vale, wondering what to do, and he sees me, I think. I start toward him, but he gives a subtle shake of his head. He continues talking to the guard, slipping one hand in his coat to ease a gun out and carefully place it on the ground.

Vale doesn't want me to come over there. Instead I duck inside. If all Vale did was climb up onto the roof, he'll be okay, right? They'll just make him leave or whatever? Then I remember with dread the way the Brotherhood guards treated him before, his wrists in a zip tie, and I search frantically for keys. Glancing out the window, I see they're still standing there at the edge, talking.

I yank the drawers open, my hands shaky. Inside the main, wide drawer there's a ring of keys on a key chain. I grab them and turn to leave, edging around the back of the building.

In order to get to the stairs and try the keys, I'll be out in the open. The guard's back is to me but there's no guarantee he won't hear me or see me. I should go, just take the laptop and make my way as carefully as I can to the stairs.

The thought of leaving Vale still tugs at me. What if we could get away together, and I could somehow get the laptop to the PS without him realizing? The thing is, they'll still want me to go back to the PS and he'll be here. We won't be together either way, and he's probably safer without me.

I might be able to slip away and he won't know for sure that I was a spy for the PS. He could think I left. Something in my stomach tells me he'll know, he'll figure it out, and his father too. But I can hope. Maybe he'll think I took off for New England or the West Coast. That I'm off somewhere, swimming free.

Their voices murmur as I step out and move toward the stairs. Vale is talking to the man, trying to keep him distracted while I get over to the stairwell. Just a little farther and I can get the door open, and maybe he can get out behind me.

I reach the door. Too nervous to glance behind me, I try the keys with trembling hands. Before I can find one that fits, the door pushes open suddenly, knocking me back. Stunned, I fall, my face burning where the metal door hit me.

There are boots everywhere as men pour out of the stairwell.

"Ami," I hear Vale yell, and I roll to my side, moaning. I push myself to my knees as Vale runs to me, but there's an unfamiliar hand closing around my arm, jerking me to my feet. Jeremy, the guy we talked to earlier, has a grip on me, and a gun in his other hand, pointed at the ground.

"Get your hands off her," Vale snarls. Jeremy lets go but smiles, calm and scary. There's half a dozen men now, all with guns. Vale's gun is still back at the edge of the roof, and there are three men standing in front of the door. I wonder what would happen if I ran for the ladder at the side of the roof. They'd shoot me. That's how it works up here, right? Shoot first, ask questions later.

Jeremy wipes sweat away from the corner of his forehead with the back of his hand. They must have run up all the stairs.

"Well, well, imagine this. My honored guests, up here

on the roof." His eyes dart around, as if looking for someone else. There's a noise, an alert from his pocket, and he checks his phone.

He stares down at the phone and types something back, exchanging a smirk with the guard next to him.

"Let's just see what our friends have been up to, shall we? Hand over the backpack, my dear Anna," Jeremy says, getting my name wrong.

I stare at Vale but there are no answers in his eyes. I take in one man after another, all the guns trained on us. I have no choice. I hand him the backpack.

Vale makes a noise in his throat and Jeremy unzips the backpack, grinning wider than ever.

"Ah, a laptop," he says. I don't understand why he's smiling so widely.

"It was me," Vale says, from where he stands. "She was just doing what I told her to do."

I know what he's up to but I don't want that. I don't want him to take the fall for me. Not when I was planning to leave him up here.

"No, I—"

"Don't listen to her. She's just my girlfriend. Let her go."

Jeremy cocks his head. He's handsome, his blond hair curling around his ears in a way that would make girls back at my high school sigh, but the way he's acting has me more nervous than ever. He pulls his phone out again.

"Just a little longer," he says.

Vale's eyes dart around, no doubt wondering what I'm wondering. A little longer until what? We all stand here.

Jeremy, that stupid grin plastered on his face, holds the backpack with the laptop. His fingers tap on the edge of the zipper. The guards stand stiffly with their guns out, silently waiting.

"Jeremy," Vale says, low and urgent. "Just let her go, she's not involved."

"She's obviously involved," Jeremy scoffs. "But I wouldn't worry so much about your girlfriend if I were you. I would worry about yourself."

And weirdly, a flash of fear flickers through Jeremy's eyes. My stomach drops. He's the one with the guns trained on us, what does he have to fear? Maybe Vale was able to call for backup from the Forge?

With that, the stairs echo with footsteps. This time it's not a mad rush of boots, but the footsteps are lighter, the rhythms precise. I stiffen.

The sound of it, the tap of feet all together in perfect rhythm. I heard it at school when the CSOs came to talk to us about Clearance and job opportunities. I heard it when Mom used to take me to work on days off school.

I heard it at Security headquarters, at a daycare for the babies of the Officers. I went to help out the caregivers and get my babysitting license. I'd walk up and down the long room with a baby on my shoulder, looking through the clear glass that showed the gymnasium down below where they trained.

The gym was enormous and the Officers would do their morning jog, their boots a steady rhythm on the floor. The sound echoed through the glass, where I could feel it in my body. It was the same tap, tap, tap. The same steady tempo, every day.

Some days I'd be walking a baby in a carrier, other days carrying a lonely two-year-old or bouncing a playful toddler.

But the steady drum of their jogging during their warm-up was always the same, and that's what I hear, coming up the stairs, steady and true.

NEW YORK TIMES *LETTERS TO THE EDITOR*

AUGUST 14, 2025

One year after the bombing near Tehran, Iran, we're all still mourning the loss of life from that terrible attack ("Anniversary of nuclear bomb dropped in Iran marked with silence and memorials worldwide"). I'm grateful for the nations that have come together to sign the Universal Accord.

The Earth has always been a home for *some* people to live their lives in peace, but never for every single human to do so. People Against Violence has changed that, with the cooperation of our banking and communications partners.

Now that peace is spreading to all corners of the Earth, we must remember the words that founded Mothers Against Violence. We all made a pledge of nonviolence from our very first meeting. These are the words we spoke when we joined the group: *"My heart is with the safety of all people. Killing is a choice I choose not to make."*

I write this letter from the town of Najafabad in Iran. I'm concerned about the plans for finishing the "Integration" as our leaders call it. What does PAV intend for the tunnels of Gaza? What will they do with the nuclear plants in Iran and North Korea that refuse to dismantle?

I urge all members of PAV to advocate that these final cells of combatants be dealt with humanely. We must not abandon our peaceful ideals. To value human life is to value all lives, including the men who refuse to comply with the Universal Accord.

Sincerely,
Mikayla Adamson

34

VALE

AFTER THE FIGHT

I WAS FEELING PRETTY optimistic until the moment I looked up, halfway up the wall, and saw the head sticking out over the edge at the top, staring down silently.

It wasn't Ami. My stomach sunk. Did they catch her? What's going on up there? I couldn't climb back down and abandon her. Besides, I bet that guy called for reinforcements at the bottom.

I got to the top and pulled myself over. It was like that scene in *The Princess Bride*, but this guy didn't go easy and start with playful sparring. He's currently got a gun trained on me. They're going to take me to a back room and beat me until I tell them what I'm doing here. That's the best-case scenario.

And it assumes Ami didn't get caught. From what the Forge saw with drones, there's not much up here besides the security office and the entrance to the stairs, and Ami said that's locked. I believe her. She wouldn't have a reason to lie about it that I can think of.

It certainly would have been easier to use the stairs than do that ridiculous boxing match. I didn't think they would appreciate me whipping one of their men, so I had to go back and forth with him.

Now my vision is compromised and I have to figure out what to do about this guard. Disarming him is the priority. Is he alone or what? He has me covered with his gun and I know the drill. I gently remove my weapon and put it on the ground between us.

Now it's his move and I wait for him to speak, running through different ways to disarm him in my head. I have the device my father gave me in my pocket. I could jam it into his neck and the meds would hit him immediately.

I scan him, the way he's holding the gun, searching for clues that this guy is scared or doesn't know what he's doing, a hesitation or tension. I don't see any. He's well trained.

"Vale Adamson," the guy says. I nod.

"And you are…"

He shakes his head, keeping the gun steady.

"Are we, uh, going to talk?" I ask as I subtly glance behind him, scanning for Ami.

He stares.

"Is that the plan? Rest of the solstice, just standing here on the roof?"

"They're coming," he finally cracks and speaks up.

I shake my head with fake sorrow. "You need backup? Yeah, I'm pretty dangerous."

He rolls his eyes, doesn't take the bait.

I see it then, the flash of someone moving into the guard office. If that's Ami, my job is to keep this guy distracted, but still disarm him so we can both get away before backup arrives, through the stairs.

They have the key after all, they'll come through there. That doesn't mean there won't also be guards at the bottom of the ladder, but we'll cross that bridge when we come to it. Maybe I can call for backup from the Forge to help us get out on the ground level.

"So, enjoying your solstice?" I ask, trying to get the guy to engage with me.

He sighs.

I watch Ami creep across the roof. In the twilight she looks like a beautiful ghost drifting against the faint pink of the sunrise to come, her shadow barely visible.

I let myself stare too long and the guy turns around, but Ami's already at the stairwell, and she has keys.

His attention on Ami, I rush him, knocking the gun from his hands. It clatters off the roof and he swears. I head to the stairwell, running flat out.

I see her hands shaking. She's trying different keys until suddenly the door swings open forcefully, knocking her back.

"Ami!" The guard is right behind me. Before I can reach her, Jeremy is stepping out of the stairwell surrounded by Brotherhood guards, dragging her to her feet.

"Get your hands off her." My vision blurs further and I'm suddenly a lot less concerned about what happens to me. I need to get them away from Ami and get her out of here safely.

I try to remind myself that I'm here on a mission for the Forge, but my world narrows to Ami, me, and these guards. Without thinking I sink, infinitesimally, into a fight stance, making note of all the weapons. I can at least disarm a couple of these guys and maybe cause a big enough disturbance that she can get away while they deal with me. The stairs are right here, the door is open.

I argue with Jeremy, telling him that Ami's just my girlfriend, that they don't need her, while I decide on the order. First the jerk who cornered me by the edge of the roof, then the big guy looming over Jeremy like a bodyguard.

I'm not worried about Jeremy. He's not like me. He never has to work for anything, never has to fight and train with the others. I'm not saying my father's way was the right way, but here we are, and only one of us needs a bodyguard.

They keep talking. I'm sure he's so excited for his whole evil plan, and I'm arguing without thinking, just to keep him talking.

Then I hear the sound of footsteps on the stairs and I can tell right away they're not Brotherhood guards. They don't run like that. I would know this sound anywhere, because I went through a whole training camp when I infiltrated the PS the first time.

They're a different breed, the PS guards and soldiers. It's the conditioning they do, mentally and physically. I'll say it. It's way beyond the training at the Forge, maybe because their weapons are so limited. At least the weapons we're aware of. There's intelligence that suggests they're developing biological and chemical weapons to use against men.

My brain feels like it breaks apart as a troop of white-clad soldiers exits the door in single file, stun guns in hand, and surrounds the entire group: Ami, me, Jeremy, and his goons.

"Quite a party you all throw around here," I say dryly to Jeremy. "I assume these guests are here at your invitation?"

One of the women, pale with a long blond braid, clears her throat. "Vale Adamson, you are under arrest."

I scoff. "We're in Alaska, not Pennsylvania, in case you didn't notice. You can't arrest me here."

She looks around politely, at the number of weapons aimed at me and holds out her hand to Jeremy, gesturing for the backpack.

Ami stiffens beside me. Her face is closed up tight, the hard mask she wears when she's trying not to flinch or show any reaction. Jeremy hands over the backpack, trying to look relaxed.

There goes any chance of getting that laptop back to my father. He's going to kill me if I get out of here alive.

The blond PS soldier zips open the top of the backpack and pulls out the laptop. We were so close. She holds it up, showing me a tag from the PS.

"This is Peaceful Society equipment you were trying to steal."

I stay silent. I want to ask how she can prove I was "trying to steal" it, if Ami had it in her backpack, but they'll twist anything I say. Ami's breathing speeds up beside me.

"Amity, who does this bag belong to?" the woman asks pointedly.

Ami's voice sounds hoarse, unpracticed. "Vale," she croaks.

The soldier turns to me. "Vale Adamson. You are charged with stealing Peaceful Society equipment and confidential information."

I aim a glare at Jeremy. "You knew!" I accuse, the accusation ripping out of me before I can stop it.

He grins widely and shrugs his shoulders. "Bummer, man, after everything you and your girlfriend went through, it turned out to be PS equipment."

"Does the Brotherhood agree to extradition?" the woman asks him.

"Yes, Tessa, we certainly do," Jeremy says immediately.

"What?" Ami's finally speaking up now. She coughs a little, clearing her throat. "What? You're taking him? Just— you have the laptop back—he's...."

Tessa stares at Ami and doesn't answer right away.

"Amity, it's okay," she says to Ami gently. "You did well. Your mission is complete."

Jeremy laughs outright at this. Ami reddens and takes a step toward me.

"Some girlfriend you got there," he crows, and his stupid bodyguards laugh.

"Vale," Ami says, reaching for my hand.

"This isn't Ami's fault. It's yours, Jeremy," I say, my eyes burning. "My father will hear about this. You want to go to war with the Forge?"

"With what? And why? Are you sticking around

Anchorage? Did you all change your mind about moving?" I grit my teeth and Tessa is quiet, taking in our words.

"You sell-out." I can't help it, I lunge for him, but his stupid bodyguard pulls him back. Ami clings to me as one of the PS soldiers steps forward and holds a Taser to my neck. That's the last thing I remember before the world spins and goes black.

35

AMITY

VALE FALLS WITH A THUD, his body sprawling against the black gravel of the roof. Buzzing fills my ears. I look around to see if there's an aircraft somewhere, but there's nothing. Only the Security Officer, Tessa, with her long blond braid, straightening with a satisfied look on her face. She nods to me.

"Good work, Bloome."

Jeremy turns to me in surprise, recognizing the last name. His men shift back, clustering next to the stairs. Putting themselves on one side, leaving me with the CSOs, Vale's body between us. I guess the Brotherhood was working with the PS, but why? And what has Vale done to make so many enemies?

I want to crouch down, to see if he's okay, but their eyes are sharp on me. I count and count, I slow the intake of air to my lungs, but I'm gasping, my emotions falling out of my control. I suck in the cool air, more than I need, and a wave of dizziness overtakes me.

Tessa steps forward and reaches her hand out to my shoulder.

"Okay, Amity. Okay, it's over now." She gently folds me over, my head below my heart, first-aid for hyperventilation or a panic attack.

But now I'm closer to Vale's body spread out on the ground. I waver, losing my balance as I sway. The Officer jerks me up and issues a soft command. Two women step forward, one at Vale's head and one at his feet. They bend and heft his body up, and the militia men cringe back further.

Tessa turns to them.

"We'll take him to the elevator, and you'll lead us to the back door. Our van is waiting."

Jeremy nods, his eyes wide. The guys up here all talk about their rights and how the PS is ruining everything, but they don't seem inclined to cross them, despite having guns. As the Officers disappear down the stairwell with Vale, my mind starts to clear and I stare daggers at Jeremy. Feeling my gaze, he stares back, not so cocky now.

"You sold him out?" I ask, keeping the question light. Pushing back the bitter edge I feel.

His men shift on their feet nervously. Jeremy clears his throat.

"Just ah—just cooperation between…"

"Between the Brotherhood and the PS?"

"Shut up, girlfriend, just go. He didn't have to come here, you didn't have to come with him." He spits on the ground. "The Forge thinks they're in charge of everything up here and we've had it. They're not the government."

Tessa nods. "Exactly." Her eyes linger on him. "Our agreement holds. You've fulfilled your side."

I follow as we take the steps to the fourth floor and the elevator and join the women holding Vale's unconscious body.

One of the Brotherhood guards gets on, pressing into a corner to keep space between himself and the clutch of CSOs. He puts a key into the control panel, pressing a button for the delivery exit.

The ride is silent, and when the door opens he scoots out and leads us down the hall, away from the door I used earlier, to a back door.

Outside in the dim light there's a white van that's way too clean to be up here in Anchorage.

I don't notice much else. I'm numb as I watch them load Vale's body onto the floor of the van. Then I step forward to go after him and Tessa stops me, holding out her arm.

"Stay here with me. Now, give me your wrist."

"Where are they taking him?" I ask quickly as I comply, holding out my right arm.

She pulls a SafeGuard from her pocket and a fastener and the device clicks to lock onto my wrist. I watch her dispassionately, waiting for an answer.

Instead of answering, she asks me, "Do you know what was on that laptop, Amity?"

"Um, my mom said it was plans that could allow the Forge to attack Greater Maryland."

She smiles gently.

"There was nothing. But they thought they were getting

plans for our communications systems, electric grid, and water supply."

Water supply? My stomach drops. The back door of the van swings open and a woman steps back out, handing something small to Tessa with a murmur.

Tessa examines it and then shows me.

"And he had this in his pocket." It's a device for delivering a quick shot of disabling drugs. I recognize it immediately.

"Who do you think this was for? His buddies?" she asks, and answers her own question. "It was for you."

"No. He wasn't like that. Isaiah and the Forge may have been planning stuff, but Vale wasn't like that. He tried to protect me."

Tessa smiles sympathetically. "And maybe in his own way, he did. There's a helicopter waiting for you at the airport. You're heading back to Maryland."

"Vale?" I ask

"He'll be detained. It's an option of last resort, but we need him in our jurisdiction. To keep Maryland safe, and to have more leverage over his father."

Tessa continues briskly. "He'll be okay. The men in the camps are not mistreated. Now come on, we're behind schedule."

Something's rising in me, like I'm going to scream or throw up. She says he'll be okay but I know the Society is not worried about Vale, they're thinking about the public good.

Vale was acting on what he thought was right, what he was taught by his father. Vale didn't leave me. Even at the end, he was trying to take the blame with Jeremy, trying to get them to let me go. Something inside me snaps and I push past her.

"I need to go with him. Let me in there." I lunge for the back of the van and try to shove past the woman sitting on the bench. "Take me too," I gasp. "I'll go back, but I need to stay with him."

Tessa is at the door of the van, her expression hardening. She speaks to me like a child.

"Amity Bloome, listen to me now. We have different transportation for you." The girl next to me, not much older than me, grabs my arms and stands up to pull me out of the van.

"No." I dig my heels in. "What harm can it do?" I must still have pull. "I want to stay!" My voice is shrill. "Ask my mother, call her," I demand.

Tessa frowns. "You can speak to her yourself when you get to the airport."

My mother is here? I reel, taking in this information. Why didn't she tell me? They take advantage and drag me out of the van while I struggle. They're so strong.

"Stop it," Tessa snaps. "You could be disciplined for this. You think this is how a girl in HighClear behaves?"

"What's the harm in letting me stay with him?" I cry out, shoving against the women who are restraining me.

She shushes me, glancing around. "We'll talk about it with your mom, like I said."

I yank an arm free and pull toward the van even as Tessa shuts the door and pounds on it. It pulls away. The girls holding me are strong, but I throw an elbow into one and she doubles over.

"Get off me!" There's command in my voice, strength that wasn't there before I came here. Before I went to Oath Day with Zeph and ended up mixed up in this mess. I take a swing at the other girl but she ducks and holds me tight.

They let go finally when another car drives up. Tessa opens the back door and turns to me. Her voice is flat now. "Get in. I'll be reporting your behavior to your mother and your commander."

"I don't care," I snap back. My control is still out of reach, far from the place I can snatch it back and stop myself from responding. I get in sullenly and one of the CSOs slides in beside me. Tessa speaks to her before she closes the door.

"She needs to be delivered to the airport, to the care of Calista Bloome. If she resists," she looks over at me, "subdue her." She says the words clearly and they are obviously meant for me. Then she slams the door, frustrated, and we pull away from the Brotherhood.

The girl next to me takes note of my still heaving breaths. "Amity," she says in a low voice, too quiet for the woman in the front of the car to hear. I'm not going to face her, but I turn my head a little bit in angry acknowledgment.

"They're taking him to Frederick. The camps are in Frederick," she whispers. The Institute is also near Frederick. "It's not over, you can find him there, try to help him."

I glance up fully now, narrowing my eyes at her mistrustfully.

"They have my brother too," she continues. "In the camps."

I give her a slight nod and turn away to rest my forehead against the cool pane of the window, watching the sad storefronts slide by.

36

AMITY

HALF AN HOUR ago I felt a fire burning inside me. I felt more energy, more righteous anger and aggression than I ever remember feeling.

Now my body feels heavy, each leg swinging out of the car at a crawl.

I'm having trouble keeping my eyes open. My body has decided the best way to deal with the prospect of meeting my mother at the airport is to shut down.

When the car stops, the young Officer gets out behind me and slips an arm under my shoulder, bracing me up. I'm too tired to cringe away from her touch. I sag against her as she flashes me a worried glance.

"Come on, Amity, perk up," she mutters to me.

My head rolls and hangs. I'm not trying to be dramatic, my neck just got overwhelmed holding it up.

The girl bumps her hip against me sharply and bends forward to put her face right in front of mine.

"Amity!" she whispers, loud and furious and sharp.

I jerk upright.

She widens her eyes at me significantly. "You are Amity Bloome," she begins. "You just completed your mission. Now sell it." Like we've all been trained to do, like I've done with my little brother, Ethan, and my mother has done with me, she exaggerates her breathing. Slows it, straightening upright.

By force of habit and years of training I follow along, pulling the breath longer and deeper into my lungs, finding the strength to copy her and stand up straight.

Now we're upright, facing each other. I scan around us, at the front of the black car next to scrubby grass and gravel stretching out to pine trees and white-capped mountains in the distance. A high chain-link fence with razor wire towers next to us. I glance along the fence and see there's a wide gate behind us and next to it the paved edge of one of the runways.

The young CSO uses an entirely different voice now. "Ms. Bloome, follow me, please."

I follow her to the gate. It's not morning yet, but the sun is about to come up.

I move through the opening, feeling like a tiny speck in the wide valley. Everything is so big up here. Am I getting nostalgic for Anchorage? I think suddenly of Ren and wonder how they knew. Maybe my mother will let me send them a message. I think of the pile of clothes they gave me, and my knives in the bag Tessa confiscated. Inside my jacket pocket sits Ren's folded note.

We walk across the pavement to a small cluster of people. My mom's not in white for once; instead, she's in dark flight clothes, standing next to a couple of other women.

"Amity, come here," my mother greets me warmly, holding her arms out for a hug. The young Officer has gotten me upright, but the numb, heavy feeling is still there inside me.

"Mom." I can't put the same warmth in my voice. I move forward, letting her hug me. As she reaches out to take my hand I'm vaguely aware I should seem happier to be here, to be going home. That I should be glad to be done with this mission, but I can't pretend.

A shadow of worry passes over her face but she smooths it away immediately.

"Amity, this is Officer Taylor and Officer Reed," she says, stepping back, still holding my hand. The helicopter looms out behind them, painted in camouflage, sitting on tiny wheels.

"This is my daughter, Amity Bloome."

"The arrest has been made?" Officer Reed asks.

"Yes. All facets of the mission have been successfully completed," my mother tells her, a hint of pride in her voice.

"His detention is confirmed?"

They're talking about Vale. Was this whole mission about Vale? I thought I was coming up here for Zeph. I thought they wanted me to get that laptop for the PS, but maybe Vale was the target all along. I played right into it, getting to know him, getting him to trust me.

A wave of cynicism washes over me and I realize they're still talking. He's in "secure transport," probably passed out and chained in the back of the van, the way I last saw him.

"Congratulations, Amity." The Officers are shaking my hand. Then they step aside and give a sign to the pilot of the helicopter.

"They're ready for you. We'll see you back in Maryland," Officer Taylor says to my mom. I don't know if there is something else I'm supposed to say or do so I give them a tight "thanks" and follow my mother to the door, awkwardly grasping a handle and copying her, pulling myself up into the cab.

When we are both sitting in the second row, a fourth woman, the young CSO who sat in the back of the car with me, climbs into the copilot seat and pulls on headphones with a microphone that snakes around in front of her face. My mom hands me an identical headset, donning her own.

I finish strapping in, thinking unexpectedly of Vale and the seatbelt in the car on the way to the party, and then there's a roar as the motor is turned on and the blades start up.

Outside the window, unexpectedly, a sharp movement has both me and my mother flinching away, but it's not an attack. It's a flock of red-winged blackbirds.

The flock takes to the sky against the rising sun in a wavering, undulating crowd. They're flying away from the wind and the noise of the helicopter in a churning mass, rising high. I watch as individual birds break free of the flock and then are pulled back in as the flock rises and falls through the air.

"Just a second," a woman speaks in my ear, and I startle, not recognizing the voice. It's the pilot.

"Let's let them get out of the way," she says.

The flock has moved but still swirls in the air. So many birds, maybe more than I have ever seen. The helicopter confuses them.

Now it's my mother speaking in my ear and her voice is tight.

"We're already behind schedule."

The pilot acknowledges her.

I don't know if they can hear me through the headphones if I talk, but I plead anyway, "Just wait a minute. Let them get away."

My mom reaches over and takes my hand, squeezing it. The flock is breaking away now, dipping away from the airport, heading to settle somewhere nearby.

The last couple of birds follow in pursuit and the pilot's voice returns.

"We're clear. Prepare for takeoff."

"Are we going home?" I ask my mom and her mouth tightens. I guess that's a no. I don't get to see Dad or Ethan?

"We're going straight to Frederick. You'll be debriefed there. You can finish up with Intelligence and then begin HighClear training immediately."

"What about Dad?" I mumble. It wasn't my choice to come up here, leaving without saying goodbye to him. I miss him.

"There's a break coming up," she says, "for the summer. You'll get to see him then."

"What about Zeph?" I ask.

My mom's eyes dart around and then back to me. She shakes her head. "We'll discuss it in debrief."

Below, the ground drops away, the airport growing smaller. The buildings shrink to a tiny size, with miniature cars on tiny streets, until it's only clouds, broken up by the mountains poking through. My mother settles back, her face blank, for what I assume is going to be many, many hours of travel.

I slip my cold hands into my pockets and feel the folded-up paper that Ren gave me. The city limits end and we begin flying over the endless terrain of brown and pale green ground, the plains of Canada, interspersed with mountains and lakes, as we make our return to Greater Maryland and the Peaceful Society.

Thank you so much for reading Privilege, the first book in the Peaceful Society trilogy! Look for the second book, Prisoner, in December of 2025 and the final book in 2026.

My books are brain-made. I do not use AI to write any part of my books, including drafts and outlines. I have a human editor and proofreader.

I posted some videos of me diving into the weeds of MAV and Peaceful Society lore. They are on YouTube, Instagram, and TikTok.

So find me there or on Goodreads, or join my mailing list.

-Meg

meganwobus@gmail.com

meganwobus.com

MOTHERS AGAINST VIOLENCE PLEDGE

I pledge to support the victims of violence.
My heart is with the safety of all people.
Killing is a choice I choose not to make.
My contribution is essential, my legacy will be peace.

THE UNIVERSAL ACCORD

There is a right to food, shelter, healthcare, and the choices of one's person.
There is a right to safety, dignity, and education in childhood.
Equal and universal rights are to be applied without discrimination.
No person shall own, manufacture, or operate a tool of killing.
No government shall maintain a military with deadly weapons or offensive capabilities.
No person shall be killed or tortured or held in slavery.
No person shall be detained or confined without a fair hearing.

THE COMMON OATH

I am a citizen of the Peaceful Society
I reject violence in all forms
My freedom is a Privilege
My legacy is peace

TIMELINE

- **2015** *Mothers Against Violence forms a network in cities and towns across the US. Members make a pledge of personal nonviolence.*
- **2016** *Baltimore chapter forms, focusing on supporting the victims of violence.*
- **2017** *Congress passes the Commonsense Gun Guidelines bill with MAV support requiring universal trigger locks and background checks.*
- **2018** *Maryland passes the Update to Gun Licensing bill in the state legislature creating strict rules for buying and carrying a gun in Maryland. The 28th Amendment, a repeal of the 2nd Amendment, passes Congress and goes to the states for ratification.*
- **2019** *The 28th Amendment is ratified, repealing the right to own and carry a gun. Congress passes a nationwide gun control bill that bans semi-automatic weapons and places restrictions on public carry. The*

name of the organization is changed to People Against
Violence. Gun buybacks begin.

- **2020** The Halt Weapons Sales bill is passed in
  Congress, stopping the manufacture and sale of weapons
  abroad.
- **2021** Police in the US are banned from carrying guns
  except for special units. All public carry is outlawed, and
  metal detectors check for guns in most public buildings.
- **2022** The People Against Violence Party wins a
  majority of seats in the US elections. Worldwide, more
  governments move to stop the sale of weapons and
  defund their militaries.
- **2024** Religious Extremists steal a nuclear warhead and
  drop it near the city of Tehran, causing widespread
  destruction and taking millions of lives. This results in
  banks, tech, and communications companies joining
  with the United Nations to sign the Universal Accord,
  outlawing all weapons and requiring the dismantling of
  militaries.
- **2025** The fight to force the last groups to disarm is
  called the Integration. Selene Bloome is killed in an
  accident as a volunteer for nuclear disarmament, using
  the pit stuffing method to disarm missiles at the Tel Nof
  Airbase in Israel. Mikayla Adamson is sent to the
  nuclear facility Natanz in Iran to assist in disarmament
  and entombment of the site but disappears while there,
  presumed to be dead.
- **2026** The United States breaks into territories. The city
  governments of Baltimore, Washington, DC, and
  Philadelphia, dominated by the People Against Violence

party, combine to form the Peaceful Society of Greater Maryland. Many Rights are revoked and regranted as Privileges upon taking the Common Oath at age 18. Men's Privileges are limited.

ABOUT THE AUTHOR

Megan Wobus likes to write, but she likes to read even more. Sometimes she plays the fiddle or goes hiking, but these days she's often found walking her dog, Silas, in her Baltimore neighborhood. There is a cat living in her basement who appears daily to demand food refills.

Megan's husband, Charley, plays the banjo and the accordion, but has many other redeeming qualities. They are the parents of three very cool teenagers.

Megan dreams of writing in a little cabin in the woods, or on a beach, or a mountain, or anywhere quiet, but the truth is she works best in a Baltimore coffee shop or in her crowded rowhouse.

Megan also writes children's chapter book mysteries under the name Willow Night.

ACKNOWLEDGMENTS

I created the Peaceful Society in 2023 as a private way to process my own frustration with the world's refusal to find a way to end the manufacture and distribution of guns and weapons.

Progress in our society and our world should not be measured in dollars, or terabytes, or the capabilities of artificial intelligence or even in opportunities created in education or advancements in healthcare.

First, we must be safe, and our families and friends and our children must be safe. In my view, everything else can come after that. There is no world worth building where we kill each other in sanctioned ways.

I wrote *Privilege* for The Emily Contest hosted by the League of Romance Writers, and I'm grateful to the League. Without the contest this novel would not be here now.

Thank you to everyone who helped me along the way, including my little team of alpha readers, Diana, Emily, and Charley, and all the folks who helped with beta reading, coworking, and other suggestions. I'm especially grateful to my editor, Christine LePorte, and proofreader, Linda Wobus.

Thank you most of all to Charley, Emily, Kiva, and Lazar

for putting up with all my mishigas about writing. I love you all so much.

This book is dedicated to my late friend Brigitte Jacobson, who wrote the best letters to the editor. You can read about her and contribute to her work at Empowerment Though Aviation, a foundation dedicated to her memory.

THE PEACEFUL SOCIETY
TRILOGY

MEGAN WOBUS

Privilege (Book 1)
  Prisoner (Book 2)
  Book 3 Coming in 2026

Join the mailing list for occasional updates and get a bonus chapter of Privilege! www.meganwobus.com